Diana Of The Crossways Book 1

by

George Meredith

Diana Of The Crossways Book 1
by George Meredith

Copyright © 2023

All Rights reserved.
No part of this publication may be reproduced,
stored in a retrieval system, or transmitted in any
form or by any means, electronic, mechanical,
photocopying or Otherwise, without the written
permission of the publisher.

The author/editor asserts the moral right to
be identified as the author/editor of this work.

ISBN: 978-93-57484-75-6

Published by
DOUBLE 9 BOOKS
2/13-B, Ansari Road
Daryaganj, New Delhi – 110002
info@double9books.com
www.double9books.com
Tel. 011-40042856

This book is under public domain

ABOUT THE AUTHOR

George Meredith OM (February 12, 1828-May 18, 1909) was born in Portsmouth, United Kingdom. He was an English poet, writer, and author, whose books are noted for their intelligence, extraordinary dialogues, and aphoristic way of writing. Meredith's books are also recognised for psychological studies of character and a highly subjective perspective on life that is a long way ahead of its time, considering women are equals to men in all streams. His most popular works are The Ordeal of Richard Feverel (1859) and The Egoist (1879). He was nominated for the Nobel Prize in Literature seven times.

CONTENTS

CHAPTER I.
OF DIARIES AND DIARISTS TOUCHING
THE HEROINE 7

CHAPTER II.
AN IRISH BALL 22

CHAPTER III.
THE INTERIOR OF MR. REDWORTH,
AND THE EXTERIOR OF MR. SULLIVAN SMITH 33

CHAPTER IV.
CONTAINING HINTS OF DIANA'S
EXPERIENCES AND OF WHAT THEY LED TO 42

CHAPTER V.
CONCERNING THE SCRUPULOUS GENTLEMAN
WHO CAME TOO LATE 54

CHAPTER VI.
THE COUPLE 63

CHAPTER VII.
THE CRISIS 71

CHAPTER VIII.
IN WHICH IS EXHIBITED HOW A
PRACTICAL MAN AND A DIVINING
WOMAN LEARN TO RESPECT ONE ANOTHER 78

CHAPTER I.
OF DIARIES AND DIARISTS TOUCHING THE HEROINE

Among the Diaries beginning with the second quarter of our century, there is frequent mention of a lady then becoming famous for her beauty and her wit: 'an unusual combination,' in the deliberate syllables of one of the writers, who is, however, not disposed to personal irony when speaking of her. It is otherwise in his case and a general fling at the sex we may deem pardonable, for doing as little harm to womankind as the stone of an urchin cast upon the bosom of mother Earth; though men must look some day to have it returned to them, which is a certainty; and indeed full surely will our idle-handed youngster too, in his riper season; be heard complaining of a strange assault of wanton missiles, coming on him he knows not whence; for we are all of us distinctly marked to get back what we give, even from the thing named inanimate nature.

The 'LEAVES FROM THE DIARY OF HENRY WILMERS' are studded with examples of the dinner-table wit of the time, not always worth quotation twice; for smart remarks have their measured distances, many requiring to be a brule pourpoint, or within throw of the pistol, to make it hit; in other words, the majority of them are addressed directly to our muscular system, and they have no effect when we stand beyond the range. On the contrary, they reflect sombrely on the springs of hilarity in the generation preceding us; with due reserve of credit, of course, to an animal vivaciousness that seems to have wanted so small an incitement. Our old yeomanry farmers—returning to their beds over ferny commons under bright moonlight from a neighbour's harvest-home, eased their bubbling breasts with a ready roar not unakin to it. Still the promptness to laugh is an excellent progenitorial foundation for the wit to come in a people; and undoubtedly the diarial record of an imputed piece of wit is witness to the spouting of laughter. This should comfort us while we skim the sparkling passages of the 'Leaves.' When a nation has acknowledged that it is as yet but in the fisticuff stage of the art of condensing our purest sense to golden sentences, a readier appreciation will be extended to the gift: which is to strike not the dazzled eyes, the unanticipating nose, the ribs, the sides, and stun us, twirl us, hoodwink, mystify, tickle and twitch, by dexterities of lingual sparring and shuffling, but to strike roots in the mind, the Hesperides of good things. We shall then set a price on the 'unusual combination.' A witty woman is a treasure; a witty Beauty is a power. Has she actual beauty, actual wit? —not simply a tidal material beauty that passes current any pretty flippancy or staggering pretentiousness? Grant. the combination, she will appear a veritable queen of her period, fit for homage; at least meriting a disposition to believe the best of her, in the teeth of foul rumour; because the well of true wit is truth itself, the gathering of the precious drops of right reason, wisdom's lightning; and no soul possessing and dispensing it can justly be a target for the world, however well armed the world confronting her. Our temporary world, that Old Credulity and stone-hurling urchin in one, supposes it possible for a woman to be mentally active up to the point of spiritual clarity and also fleshly vile; a guide to life and a biter at the fruits of death; both open mind and hypocrite. It has not yet been taught to appreciate a quality certifying to sound citizenship as authoritatively as acres of land in fee simple, or coffers of bonds, shares and stocks, and a more imperishable guarantee. The multitudes of evil reports which it takes for proof, are marshalled against her without question of the nature of the victim, her temptress beauty being a sufficiently presumptive delinquent. It does not pretend to know the whole, or naked body of the facts; it knows enough for its furry dubiousness; and excepting the sentimental of men, a rocket-headed horde, ever at the heels of fair faces for ignition, and up starring away at a hint of tearfulness; excepting further by chance a solid champion man, or some generous woman capable of faith in the pelted solitary of her sex, our temporary world blows direct East on her shivering person. The scandal is warrant for that; the circumstances of the scandal emphasize the warrant. And how clever she is! Cleverness is an attribute of the selecter missionary lieutenants of Satan. We pray to be defended from her cleverness: she flashes bits of speech that catch men in their unguarded corner. The wary stuff their ears, the stolid bid her best sayings rebound on her reputation. Nevertheless the world, as Christian, remembers its professions, and a portion of it joins the burly in morals by extending to her a rough old charitable mercifulness; better than sentimental ointment, but the heaviest blow she has to bear, to a character swimming for life.

That the lady in question was much quoted, the Diaries and Memoirs testify. Hearsay as well as hearing was at work to produce the abundance; and it was a novelty in England, where (in company) the men are the pointed talkers, and the women conversationally fair Circassians. They are, or they know that they should be; it comes to the same. Happily our civilization has not prescribed the veil to them. The mutes have here and there a sketch or label attached to their names: they are 'strikingly handsome'; they are 'very good-looking'; occasionally they are noted as 'extremely entertaining': in what manner, is inquired by a curious posterity, that in so many matters is left unendingly to jump the empty and gaping figure of interrogation over its own full stop. Great ladies must they be, at the web of politics, for us to hear them cited discoursing. Henry Wilmers is not content to quote the beautiful Mrs. Warwick, he attempts a portrait. Mrs. Warwick is 'quite Grecian.' She might 'pose for a statue.' He presents her in carpenter's lines, with a dab of school-box colours, effective to those whom the Keepsake fashion can stir. She has a straight nose, red lips, raven hair, black eyes, rich complexion, a remarkably fine bust, and she walks well, and has an agreeable voice; likewise 'delicate extremities.' The writer was created for popularity, had he chosen to bring his art into our literary market.

Perry Wilkinson is not so elaborate: he describes her in his 'Recollections' as a splendid brune, eclipsing all the blondes coming near her: and 'what is more, the beautiful creature can talk.' He wondered, for she was young, new to society. Subsequently he is rather ashamed of his wonderment, and accounts for it by 'not having known she was Irish.' She 'turns out to be Dan Merion's daughter.'

We may assume that he would have heard if she had any whiff of a brogue. Her sounding of the letter R a trifle scrupulously is noticed by Lady Pennon: 'And last, not least, the lovely Mrs. Warwick, twenty minutes behind the dinner-hour, and r-r-really fearing she was late.'

After alluding to the soft influence of her beauty and ingenuousness on the vexed hostess, the kindly old marchioness adds, that it was no wonder she was late, 'for just before starting from home she had broken loose from her husband for good, and she entered the room absolutely houseless!' She was not the less 'astonishingly brilliant.' Her observations were often 'so unexpectedly droll I laughed till I cried.' Lady Pennon became in consequence one of the stanch supporters of Mrs. Warwick.

Others were not so easily won. Perry Wilkinson holds a balance when it goes beyond a question of her wit and beauty. Henry Wilmers puts the case aside, and takes her as he finds her. His cousin, the clever and cynical Dorset Wilmers, whose method of conveying his opinions without stating them was famous, repeats on two occasions when her name appears in his pages, 'handsome, lively, witty'; and the stressed repetition of calculated brevity while a fiery scandal was abroad concerning the lady, implies weighty substance—the reservation of a constable's truncheon, that could legally have knocked her character down to the pavement. We have not to ask what he judged. But Dorset Wilmers was a political opponent of the eminent Peer who yields the second name to the scandal, and politics in his day flushed the conceptions of men. His short references to 'that Warwick-Dannisburgh affair' are not verbally malicious. He gets wind of the terms of Lord Dannisburgh's will and testament, noting them without comment. The oddness of the instrument in one respect may have served his turn; we have no grounds for thinking him malignant. The death of his enemy closes his allusions to Mrs. Warwick. He was growing ancient, and gout narrowed the circle he whirled in. Had he known this 'handsome, lively, witty' apparition as a woman having political and social views of her own, he would not, one fancies, have been so stingless. Our England exposes a sorry figure in his Reminiscences. He struck heavily, round and about him, wherever he moved; he had by nature a tarnishing eye that cast discolouration. His unadorned harsh substantive statements, excluding the adjectives, give his Memoirs the appearance of a body of facts, attractive to the historic Muse, which has learnt to esteem those brawny sturdy giants marching club on shoulder, independent of henchman, in preference to your panoplied knights with their puffy squires, once her favourites, and wind-filling to her columns, ultimately found indigestible.

His exhibition of his enemy Lord Dannisburgh, is of the class of noble portraits we see swinging over inn-portals, grossly unlike in likeness. The possibility of the man's doing or saying this and that adumbrates the improbability: he had something of the character capable of it, too much good sense for the performance. We would think so, and still the shadow is round our thoughts. Lord Dannisburgh was a man of ministerial tact, official ability, Pagan morality; an excellent general manager, if no genius in statecraft. But he was careless of social opinion, unbuttoned, and a laugher. We know that he could be chivalrous toward women, notwithstanding the perplexities he brought on them, and this the Dorset- Diary does not show.

His chronicle is less mischievous as regards Mrs. Warwick than the paragraphs of Perry Wilkinson, a gossip presenting an image of perpetual chatter, like the waxen-faced street advertizements of light and easy dentistry. He has no belief, no disbelief; names the proparty and the con; recites the case, and discreetly, over-discreetly; and pictures the trial, tells the list of witnesses, records the verdict: so the case went, and some thought one thing, some another thing: only it is reported for positive that a miniature of the incriminated lady was cleverly smuggled over to the jury, and juries sitting upon these eases, ever since their bedazzlement by Phryne, as you know . . . . And then he relates an anecdote of the husband, said to have been not a bad fellow before he married his Diana; and the naming of the Goddess reminds him that the second person in the indictment is now everywhere called 'The elderly shepherd';—but immediately after the bridal bells this husband became sour and insupportable, and either she had the trick of putting him publicly in the wrong, or he lost all shame in playing the churlish domestic tyrant. The instances are incredible of a gentleman. Perry Wilkinson gives us two or three; one on the authority of a personal friend who witnessed the scene; at the Warwick whist-table, where the fair Diana would let loose her silvery laugh in the intervals. She was hardly out of her teens, and should have been dancing instead of fastened to a table. A difference of fifteen years in the ages of the wedded pair accounts poorly for the husband's conduct, however solemn a business the game of whist. We read that he burst out at last, with bitter mimicry, 'yang—yang—yang!' and killed the bright laugh, shot it dead. She had outraged the decorum of the square-table only while the cards were making. Perhaps her too-dead ensuing silence, as of one striving to bring back the throbs to a slain bird in her bosom, allowed the gap between the wedded pair to be visible, for it was dated back to prophecy as soon as the trumpet proclaimed it.

But a multiplication of similar instances, which can serve no other purpose than that of an apology, is a miserable vindication of innocence. The more we have of them the darker the inference. In delicate situations the chatterer is noxious. Mrs. Warwick had numerous apologists. Those trusting to her perfect rectitude were rarer. The liberty she allowed herself in speech and action must have been trying to her defenders in a land like ours; for here, and able to throw its shadow on our giddy upper-circle, the rigour of the game of life, relaxed though it may sometimes appear, would satisfy the staidest whist-player. She did not wish it the reverse, even when claiming a space for laughter: 'the breath of her soul,' as she called it, and as it may be felt in the early youth of a lively nature. She, especially, with her multitude of quick perceptions and imaginative avenues, her rapid summaries, her sense of the comic, demanded this aerial freedom.

We have it from Perry Wilkinson that the union of the divergent couple was likened to another union always in a Court of Law. There was a distinction; most analogies will furnish one; and here we see England and Ireland changeing their parts, until later, after the breach, when the Englishman and Irishwoman resumed a certain resemblance to the yoked Islands.

Henry Wilmers, I have said, deals exclusively with the wit and charm of the woman. He treats the scandal as we might do in like manner if her story had not to be told. But these are not reporting columns; very little of it shall trouble them. The position is faced, and that is all. The position is one of the battles incident to women, their hardest. It asks for more than justice from men, for generosity, our civilization not being yet of the purest. That cry of hounds at her disrobing by Law is instinctive. She runs, and they give tongue; she is a creature of the chase. Let her escape unmangled, it will pass in the record that she did once publicly run, and some old dogs will persist in thinking her cunninger than the virtuous, which never put themselves in such positions, but ply the distaff at home. Never should reputation of woman trail a scent! How true! and true also that the women of waxwork never do; and that the women of happy marriages do not; nor the women of holy nunneries; nor the women lucky in their arts. It is a test of the civilized to see and hear, and add no yapping to the spectacle.

Thousands have reflected on a Diarist's power to cancel our Burial Service. Not alone the cleric's good work is upset by him; but the sexton's as well. He howks the grave, and transforms the quiet worms, busy on a single poor peaceable body, into winged serpents that disorder sky and earth with a deadly flight of zig-zags, like military rockets, among the living. And if these are given to cry too much, to have their tender sentiments considered, it cannot be said that History requires the flaying of them. A gouty Diarist, a sheer gossip Diarist, may thus, in the bequest of a trail of reminiscences, explode our temples (for our very temples have powder in store), our treasuries, our homesteads, alive with dynamitic stuff; nay, disconcert our inherited veneration, dislocate the intimate connexion between the tugged flaxen forelock and a title.

No similar blame is incurred by Henry Wilmers. No blame whatever, one would say, if he had been less, copious, or not so subservient, in recording the lady's utterances; for though the wit of a woman may be terse, quite spontaneous, as this lady's assuredly was here and there, she is apt to spin it out of a museful mind, at her toilette, or by the lonely fire, and sometimes it is imitative; admirers should beware of holding it up to the withering glare of print: she herself, quoting an obscure maximmonger, says of these lapidary sentences, that they have merely 'the value of chalk-eggs, which lure the thinker to sit,' and tempt the vacuous to strain for the like, one might add; besides flattering the world to imagine itself richer than it is in eggs that are golden. Henry Wilmers notes a multitude of them. 'The talk fell upon our being creatures of habit, and how far it was good: She said:— It is there that we see ourselves crutched between love grown old and indifference ageing to love.' Critic ears not present at the conversation catch an echo of maxims and aphorisms overchannel, notwithstanding a feminine thrill in the irony of 'ageing to love.' The quotation ranks rather among the testimonies to her charm.

She is fresher when speaking of the war of the sexes. For one sentence out of many, though we find it to be but the clever literary clothing of a common accusation: 'Men may have rounded Seraglio Point: they have not yet doubled Cape Turk.'

It is war, and on the male side, Ottoman war: her experience reduced her to think so positively. Her main personal experience was in the social class which is primitively venatorial still, canine under its polish.

She held a brief for her beloved Ireland. She closes a discussion upon Irish agitation by saying rather neatly: 'You have taught them it is English as well as common human nature to feel an interest in the dog that has bitten you.'

The dog periodically puts on madness to win attention; we gather then that England, in an angry tremour, tries him with water-gruel to prove him sane.

Of the Irish priest (and she was not of his retinue), when he was deemed a revolutionary, Henry Wilmers notes her saying: 'Be in tune with him; he is in the key-note for harmony. He is shepherd, doctor, nurse, comforter, anecdotist and fun-maker to his poor flock; and you wonder they see the burning gateway of their heaven in him? Conciliate the priest.'

It has been partly done, done late, when the poor flock have found their doctoring and shepherding at other hands: their 'bulb-food and fiddle,' that she petitioned for, to keep them from a complete shaving off their patch of bog and scrub soil, without any perception of the tremulous transatlantic magnification of the fiddle, and the splitting discord of its latest inspiriting jig.

And she will not have the consequences of the 'weariful old Irish duel between Honour and Hunger judged by bread and butter juries.'

She had need to be beautiful to be tolerable in days when Englishmen stood more openly for the strong arm to maintain the Union. Her troop of enemies was of her summoning.

Ordinarily her topics were of wider range, and those of a woman who mixed hearing with reading, and observation with her musings. She has no doleful ejaculatory notes, of the kind peculiar to women at war, containing one-third of speculative substance to two of sentimental — a feminine plea for comprehension and a squire; and it was probably the reason (as there is no reason to suppose an emotional cause) why she exercised her evident sway over the mind of so plain and straightforward an Englishman as Henry Wilmers. She told him that she read rapidly, 'a great deal at one gulp,' and thought in flashes—a way with the makers of phrases. She wrote, she confessed, laboriously. The desire to prune, compress, overcharge, was a torment to the nervous woman writing under a sharp necessity for payment. Her songs were shot off on the impulsion; prose was the heavy task. 'To be pointedly rational,' she said, 'is a greater difficulty for me than a fine delirium.' She did not talk as if it would have been so, he remarks. One is not astonished at her appearing an 'actress' to the flat-minded. But the basis of her woman's nature was pointed flame: In the fulness of her history we perceive nothing histrionic. Capricious or enthusiastic in her youth, she never trifled with feeling; and if she did so with some showy phrases and occasionally proffered commonplaces in gilt, as she was much excited to do, her moods of reflection were direct, always large and honest, universal as well as feminine.

Her saying that 'A woman in the pillory restores the original bark of brotherhood to mankind,' is no more than a cry of personal anguish. She has golden apples in her apron. She says of life: 'When I fail to cherish it in every fibre the fires within are waning,' and that drives like rain to the roots. She says of the world, generously, if with tapering idea: 'From the point of vision of the angels, this ugly monster, only half out of slime, must appear our one constant hero.' It can be read maliciously, but abstain.

She says of Romance: 'The young who avoid that region escape the title of Fool at the cost of a celestial crown.' Of Poetry: 'Those that have souls meet their fellows there.'

But she would have us away with sentimentalism. Sentimental people, in her phrase, 'fiddle harmonics on the strings of sensualism,' to the delight of a world gaping for marvels of musical execution rather than for music. For our world is all but a sensational world at present, in maternal travail of a soberer, a braver, a brighter-eyed. Her reflections are thus to be interpreted, it seems to me. She says, 'The vices of the world's nobler half in this day are feminine.' We have to guard against 'half-conceptions of wisdom, hysterical goodness, an impatient charity'—against the elementary state of the altruistic virtues, distinguishable as the sickness and writhings of our egoism to cast its first slough. Idea is there. The funny part of it is our finding it in books of fiction composed for payment. Manifestly this lady did not 'chameleon' her pen from the colour of her audience: she was not of the uniformed rank and file marching to drum and fife as gallant interpreters of popular appetite, and going or gone to soundlessness and the icy shades.

Touches inward are not absent: 'To have the sense of the eternal in life is a short flight for the soul. To have had it, is the soul's vitality.' And also: 'Palliation of a sin is the hunted creature's refuge and final temptation. Our battle is ever between spirit and flesh. Spirit must brand the flesh, that it may live.'

You are entreated to repress alarm. She was by preference light-handed; and her saying of oratory, that 'It is always the more impressive for the spice of temper which renders it untrustworthy,' is light enough. On Politics she is rhetorical and swings: she wrote to spur a junior politician: 'It is the first business of men, the school to mediocrity, to the covetously ambitious a sty, to the dullard his amphitheatre, arms of Titans to the desperately enterprising, Olympus to the genius.' What a woman thinks of women, is the test of her nature. She saw their existing posture clearly, yet believed, as men disincline to do, that they grow. She says, that 'In their judgements upon women men are females, voices of the present (sexual) dilemma.' They desire to have 'a still woman; who can make a constant society of her pins and needles.' They create by stoppage a volcano, and are amazed at its eruptiveness. 'We live alone, and do not much feel it till we are visited.' Love is presumably the visitor. Of the greater loneliness of women, she says: 'It is due to the prescribed circumscription of their minds, of which they become aware in agitation. Were the walls about them beaten down, they would understand that solitariness is a common human fate and the one chance of growth, like space for timber.' As to the sensations of women after the beating down of the walls, she owns that the multitude of the timorous would yearn in shivering affright for the old prison-nest, according to the sage prognostic of men; but the flying of a valiant few would form a vanguard. And we are informed that the beginning of a motive life with women must be in the head, equally with men (by no means a truism when she wrote). Also that 'men do not so much fear to lose the hearts of thoughtful women as their strict attention to their graces.' The present market is what men are for preserving: an observation of still reverberating force. Generally in her character of the feminine combatant there is a turn of phrase, like a dimple near the lips showing her knowledge that she was uttering but a tart measure of the truth. She had always too much lambent humour to be the dupe of the passion wherewith, as she says, 'we lash ourselves into the persuasive speech distinguishing us from the animals.'

The instances of her drollery are rather hinted by the Diarists for the benefit of those who had met her and could inhale the atmosphere at a word. Drolleries, humours, reputed witticisms, are like odours of roast meats, past with the picking of the joint. Idea is the only vital breath. They have it rarely, or it eludes the chronicler. To say of the great erratic and forsaken Lady A****, after she had accepted the consolations of Bacchus, that her name was properly signified in asterisks 'as she was now nightly an Ariadne in heaven through her God,' sounds to us a roundabout, with wit somewhere and fun nowhere. Sitting at the roast we might have thought differently. Perry Wilkinson is not happier in citing her reply to his compliment on the reviewers' unanimous eulogy of her humour and pathos:—the 'merry clown and poor pantaloon demanded of us in every work of fiction,' she says, lamenting the writer's compulsion to go on producing them for applause until it is extremest age that knocks their knees. We are informed by Lady Pennon of 'the most amusing description of the first impressions of a pretty English simpleton in Paris'; and here is an opportunity for ludicrous contrast of the French and English styles of pushing flatteries—'piping to the charmed animal,' as Mrs. Warwick terms it in another place: but Lady Pennon was acquainted with the silly woman of the piece, and found her amusement in the 'wonderful truth' of that representation.

Diarists of amusing passages are under an obligation to paint us a realistic revival of the time, or we miss the relish. The odour of the roast, and more, a slice of it is required, unless the humorous thing be preternaturally spirited to walk the earth as one immortal among a number less numerous than the mythic Gods. 'He gives good dinners,' a candid old critic said, when asked how it was that he could praise a certain poet. In an island of chills and fogs, coelum crebris imbribus ac nebulis foedum, the comic and other perceptions are dependent on the stirring of the gastric juices. And such a revival by any of us would be impolitic, were it a possible attempt, before our systems shall have been fortified by philosophy. Then may it be allowed to the Diarist simply to relate, and we can copy from him.

Then, ah! then, moreover, will the novelist's Art, now neither blushless infant nor executive man, have attained its majority. We can then be veraciously historical, honestly transcriptive. Rose-pink and dirty drab will alike have passed away. Philosophy is the foe of both, and their silly cancelling contest, perpetually renewed in a shuffle of extremes, as it always is where a phantasm falseness reigns, will no longer baffle the contemplation of natural flesh, smother no longer the soul issuing out of our incessant strife. Philosophy bids us to see that we are not so pretty as rose-pink, not so repulsive as dirty drab; and that instead of everlastingly shifting those barren aspects, the sight of ourselves is wholesome, bearable, fructifying, finally a delight. Do but perceive that we are coming to philosophy, the stride toward it will be a giant's —a century a day. And imagine the celestial refreshment of having a pure decency in the place of sham; real flesh; a soul born active, wind- beaten, but ascending. Honourable will fiction then appear; honourable, a fount of life, an aid to life, quick with our blood. Why, when you behold it you love it—and you will not encourage it?—or only when presented by dead hands? Worse than that alternative dirty drab, your recurring rose-pink is rebuked by hideous revelations of the filthy foul; for nature will force her way, and if you try to stifle her by drowning, she comes up, not the fairest part of her uppermost! Peruse your Realists—really your castigators for not having yet embraced Philosophy. As she grows in the flesh when discreetly tended, nature is unimpeachable, flower-eke, yet not too decoratively a flower; you must have her with the stem, the thorns, the roots, and the fat bedding of roses. In this fashion she grew, says historical fiction; thus does she flourish now, would say the modern transcript, reading the inner as well as exhibiting the outer.

And how may you know that you have reached to Philosophy? You touch her skirts when you share her hatred of the sham decent, her derision of sentimentalism. You are one with her when—but I would not have you a thousand years older! Get to her, if in no other way, by the sentimental route:—that very winding path, which again and again brings you round to the point of original impetus, where you have to be unwound for another whirl; your point of original impetus being the grossly material, not at all the spiritual. It is most true that sentimentalism springs from the former, merely and badly aping the latter,—fine flower, or pinnacle flame-spire, of sensualism that it is, could it do other? and accompanying the former it traverses tracts of desert here and there couching in a garden, catching with one hand at fruits, with another at colours; imagining a secret ahead, and goaded by an appetite, sustained by sheer gratifications. Fiddle in harmonics as it may, it will have these gratifications at all costs. Should none be discoverable, at once you are at the Cave of Despair, beneath the funereal orb of Glaucoma, in the thick midst of poniarded, slit-throat, rope-dependant figures, placarded across the bosom Disillusioned, Infidel, Agnostic, Miserrimus. That is the sentimental route to advancement. Spirituality does not light it; evanescent dreams: are its oil-lamps, often with wick askant in the socket.

A thousand years! You may count full many a thousand by this route before you are one with divine Philosophy. Whereas a single flight of brains will reach and embrace her; give you the savour of Truth, the right use of the senses, Reality's infinite sweetness; for these things are in philosophy; and the fiction which is the summary of actual Life, the within and without of us, is, prose or verse, plodding or soaring, philosophy's elect handmaiden. To such an end let us bend our aim to work, knowing that every form of labour, even this flimsiest, as you esteem it, should minister to growth. If in any branch of us we fail in growth, there is, you are aware, an unfailing aboriginal democratic old monster that waits to pull us down; certainly the branch, possibly the tree; and for the welfare of Life we fall. You are acutely conscious of yonder old monster when he is mouthing at you in politics. Be wary of him in the heart; especially be wary of the disrelish of brainstuff. You must feed on something. Matter that is not nourishing to brains can help to constitute nothing but the bodies which are pitched on rubbish heaps. Brainstuff is not lean stuff;—the brainstuff of fiction is internal history, and to suppose it dull is the profoundest of errors; how deep, you will understand when I tell you that it is the very football of the holiday-afternoon imps below. They kick it for pastime; they are intelligences perverted. The comic of it, the adventurous, the tragic, they make devilish, to kindle their Ogygian hilarity. But—sharply comic, adventurous, instructively tragic, it is in the interwinding with human affairs, to give a flavour of the modern day reviving that of our Poet, between whom and us yawn Time's most hollow jaws. Surely we owe a little to Time, to cheer his progress; a little to posterity, and to our country. Dozens of writers will be in at yonder yawning breach, if only perusers will rally to the philosophic standard. They are sick of the woodeny puppetry they dispense, as on a race-course to the roaring frivolous. Well, if not dozens, half-dozens; gallant pens are alive; one can speak of them in the plural. I venture to say that they would be satisfied with a dozen for audience, for a commencement. They would perish of inanition, unfed, unapplauded, amenable to the laws perchance for an assault on their last remaining pair of ears or heels, to hold them fast. But the example is the thing; sacrifices must be expected. The example might, one hopes, create a taste. A great modern writer, of clearest eye and head, now departed, capable in activity of presenting thoughtful women, thinking men, groaned over his puppetry, that he dared not animate them, flesh though they were, with the fires of positive brainstuff. He could have done it, and he is of the departed! Had he dared, he would (for he was Titan enough) have raised the Art in dignity on a level with History; to an interest surpassing the narrative of public deeds as vividly as man's heart and brain in their union excel his plain lines of action to eruption. The everlasting pantomime, suggested by Mrs. Warwick in her exclamation to Perry Wilkinson, is derided, not unrighteously, by our graver seniors. They name this Art the pasture of idiots, a method for idiotizing the entire population which has taken to reading; and which soon discovers that it can write likewise, that sort of stuff at least. The forecast may be hazarded, that if we do not speedily embrace Philosophy in fiction, the Art is doomed to extinction, under the shining multitude of its professors. They are fast capping the candle. Instead, therefore, of objurgating the timid intrusions of Philosophy, invoke her presence, I pray you. History without her is the skeleton map of events: Fiction a picture of figures modelled on no skeleton-anatomy. But each, with Philosophy in aid, blooms, and is humanly shapely. To demand of us truth to nature, excluding Philosophy, is really to bid a pumpkin caper. As much as legs are wanted for the dance, Philosophy is required to make our human nature credible and acceptable. Fiction implores you to heave a bigger breast and take her in with this heavenly preservative helpmate, her inspiration and her essence. You have to teach your imagination of the feminine image you have set up to bend your civilized knees to, that it must temper its fastidiousness, shun the grossness of the over-dainty. Or, to speak in the philosophic tongue, you must turn on yourself, resolutely track and seize that burrower, and scrub and cleanse him; by which process, during the course of it, you will arrive at the conception of the right heroical woman for you to worship: and if you prove to be of some spiritual stature, you may reach to an ideal of the heroical feminine type for the worship of mankind, an image as yet in poetic outline only, on our upper skies.

'So well do we know ourselves, that we one and all determine to know a purer,' says the heroine of my columns. Philosophy in fiction tells, among various other matters, of the perils of this intimate acquaintance with a flattering familiar in the 'purer'—a person who more than ceases to be of else to us after his ideal shall have led up men from their flint and arrowhead caverns to intercommunicative daylight. For when the fictitious creature has performed that service of helping to civilize the world, it becomes the most dangerous of delusions, causing first the individual to despise the mass, and then to join the mass in crushing the individual. Wherewith let us to our story, the froth being out of the bottle.

CHAPTER II.
AN IRISH BALL

In the Assembly Rooms of the capital city of the Sister Island there was a public Ball, to celebrate the return to Erin of a British hero of Irish blood, after his victorious Indian campaign; a mighty struggle splendidly ended; and truly could it be said that all Erin danced to meet him; but this was the pick of the dancing, past dispute the pick of the supping. Outside those halls the supping was done in Lazarus fashion, mainly through an excessive straining of the organs of hearing and vision, which imparted the readiness for more, declared by physicians to be the state inducing to sound digestion. Some one spied the figure of the hero at the window and was fed; some only to hear the tale chewed the cud of it; some told of having seen him mount the steps; and sure it was that at an hour of the night, no matter when, and never mind a drop or two of cloud, he would come down them again, and have an Irish cheer to freshen his pillow. For 'tis Ireland gives England her soldiers, her generals too. Farther away, over field and bogland, the whiskies did their excellent ancient service of watering the dry and drying the damp, to the toast of 'Lord Larrian, God bless him! he's an honour to the old country!' and a bit of a sigh to follow, hints of a story, and loud laughter, a drink, a deeper sigh, settling into conversation upon the brave Lord Larrian's deeds, and an Irish regiment he favoured—had no taste for the enemy without the backing of his 'boys.' Not he. Why, he'd never march to battle and they not handy; because when he struck he struck hard, he said. And he has a wound on the right hip and two fingers off his left hand; has bled for England, to show her what Irishmen are when they're well treated.

The fine old warrior standing at the upper end of the long saloon, tall, straight, grey-haired, martial in his aspect and decorations, was worthy to be the flag-pole for enthusiasm. His large grey eyes lightened from time to time as he ranged them over the floating couples, and dropped a word of inquiry to his aide, Captain Sir Lukin Dunstane, a good model of a cavalry officer, though somewhat a giant, equally happy with his chief in passing the troops of animated ladies under review. He named as many as were known to him. Reviewing women exquisitely attired for inspection, all variously and charmingly smiling, is a relief after the monotonous regiments of men. Ireland had done her best to present the hero of her blood an agreeable change; and he too expressed a patriotic satisfaction on hearing that the faces most admired by him were of the native isle. He looked upon one that came whirling up to him on a young officer's arm and swept off into the crowd of tops, for a considerable while before he put his customary question. She was returning on the spin when he said,

'Who is she?'

Sir Lukin did not know. 'She's a new bird; she nodded to my wife; I'll ask.'

He manoeuvred a few steps cleverly to where his wife reposed. The information he gathered for the behoof of his chief was, that the handsome creature answered to the name of Miss Merion; Irish; aged somewhere between eighteen and nineteen; a dear friend of his wife's, and he ought to have remembered her; but she was a child when he saw her last.

'Dan Merion died, I remember, about the day of my sailing for India,' said the General. 'She may be his daughter.'

The bright cynosure rounded up to him in the web of the waltz, with her dark eyes for Lady Dunstane, and vanished again among the twisting columns.

He made his way, handsomely bumped by an apologetic pair, to Lady Dunstane, beside whom a seat was vacated for him; and he trusted she had not over-fatigued herself.

'Confess,' she replied, 'you are perishing to know more than Lukin has been able to tell you. Let me hear that you admire her: it pleases me; and you shall hear what will please you as much, I promise you, General.'

'I do. Who wouldn't?' said he frankly.

'She crossed the Channel expressly to dance here tonight at the public Ball in honour of you.'

'Where she appears, the first person falls to second rank, and accepts it humbly.'

'That is grandly spoken.'

'She makes everything in the room dust round a blazing jewel.'

'She makes a poet of a soldier. Well, that you may understand how pleased I am, she is my dearest friend, though she is younger than I, as may be seen; she is the only friend I have. I nursed her when she was an infant; my father and Mr. Dan Merion were chums. We were parted by my marriage and the voyage to India. We have not yet exchanged a syllable: she was snapped up, of course, the moment she entered the room. I knew she would be a taking girl: how lovely, I did not guess. You are right, she extinguishes the others. She used to be the sprightliest of living creatures, and to judge by her letters, that has not faded. She 's in the market, General.'

Lord Larrian nodded to everything he heard, concluding with a mock doleful shake of the head. 'My poorest subaltern!' he sighed, in the theatrical but cordially melancholy style of green age viewing Cytherea's market.

His poorest subaltern was richer than he in the wherewithal to bid for such prizes.

'What is her name in addition to Merion?'

'Diana Antonia Merion. Tony to me, Diana to the world.'

'She lives over there?'

'In England, or anywhere; wherever she is taken in. She will live, I hope, chiefly with me.'

'And honest Irish?'

'Oh, she's Irish.'

'Ah!' the General was Irish to the heels that night.

Before further could be said the fair object of the dialogue came darting on a trip of little runs, both hands out, all her face one tender sparkle of a smile; and her cry proved the quality of her blood: 'Emmy! Emmy! my heart!'

'My dear Tony!

I should not have come but for the hope of seeing you here.'

Lord Larrian rose and received a hurried acknowledgement of his courtesy from the usurper of his place.

'Emmy! we might kiss and hug; we're in Ireland. I burn to! But you're not still ill, dear? Say no! That Indian fever must have gone. You do look a dash pale, my own; you're tired.'

'One dance has tired me. Why were you so late?'

'To give the others a chance? To produce a greater impression by suspense? No and no. I wrote you I was with the Pettigrews. We caught the coach, we caught the boat, we were only two hours late for the Ball; so we did wonders. And good Mrs. Pettigrew is, pining somewhere to complete her adornment. I was in the crush, spying for Emmy, when Mr. Mayor informed me it was the duty of every Irishwoman to dance her toes off, if she 'd be known for what she is. And twirl! a man had me by the waist, and I dying to find you.'

'Who was the man?'

'Not to save these limbs from the lighted stake could I tell you!'

'You are to perform a ceremonious bow to Lord Larrian.'

'Chatter first! a little!'

The plea for chatter was disregarded. It was visible that the hero of the night hung listening and in expectation. He and the Beauty were named to one another, and they chatted through a quadrille. Sir Lukin introduced a fellow-Harrovian of old days, Mr. Thomas Redworth, to his wife.

'Our weather-prophet, meteorologist,' he remarked, to set them going; 'you remember, in India, my pointing to you his name in a newspaper— letter on the subject. He was generally safe for the cricketing days.'

Lady Dunstane kindly appeared to call it to mind, and she led upon the them-queried at times by an abrupt 'Eh?' and 'I beg pardon,' for manifestly his gaze and one of his ears, if not the pair, were given to the young lady discoursing with Lord Larrian. Beauty is rare; luckily is it rare, or, judging from its effect on men, and the very stoutest of them, our world would be internally more distracted planet than we see, to the perversion of business, courtesy, rights of property, and the rest. She perceived an incipient victim, of the hundreds she anticipated, and she very tolerantly talked on: 'The weather and women have some resemblance they say. Is it true that he who reads the one can read the other?'

Lord Larrian here burst into a brave old laugh, exclaiming, 'Oh! good!'

Mr. Redworth knitted his thick brows. 'I beg pardon? Ah! women! Weather and women? No; the one point more variable in women makes all the difference.'

'Can you tell me what the General laughed at?'

The honest Englishman entered the trap with promptitude. 'She said:—who is she, may I ask you?'

Lady Dunstane mentioned her name.

Daughter of the famous Dan Merion? The young lady merited examination for her father's sake. But when reminded of her laughter-moving speech, Mr. Redworth bungled it; he owned he spoilt it, and candidly stated his inability to see the fun. 'She said, St. George's Channel in a gale ought to be called St. Patrick's—something—I missed some point. That quadrille-tune, the Pastourelle, or something . . .'

'She had experience of the Channel last night,' Lady Dunstane pursued, and they both, while in seeming converse, caught snatches from their neighbours, during a pause of the dance.

The sparkling Diana said to Lord Larrian, 'You really decline to make any of us proud women by dancing to-night?'

The General answered: 'I might do it on two stilts; I can't on one.' He touched his veteran leg.

'But surely,' said she, 'there's always an inspiration coming to it from its partner in motion, if one of them takes the step.'

He signified a woeful negative. 'My dear young lady, you say dark things to grey hairs!'

She rejoined: 'If we were over in England, and you fixed on me the stigma of saying dark things, I should never speak without being thought obscure.'

'It's because you flash too brightly for them.'

'I think it is rather the reminiscence of the tooth that received a stone when it expected candy.'

Again the General laughed; he looked pleased and warmed. 'Yes, that's their way, that's their way!' and he repeated her words to himself, diminishing their importance as he stamped them on his memory, but so heartily admiring the lovely speaker, that he considered her wit an honour to the old country, and told her so. Irish prevailed up to boiling-point.

Lady Dunstane, not less gratified, glanced up at Mr. Redworth, whose brows bore the knot of perplexity over a strong stare. He, too, stamped the words on his memory, to see subsequently whether they had a vestige of meaning. Terrifically precocious, he thought her. Lady Dunstane, in her quick sympathy with her friend, read the adverse mind in his face. And her reading of the mind was right, wrong altogether her deduction of the corresponding sentiment.

Music was resumed to confuse the hearing of the eavesdroppers.

They beheld a quaint spectacle: a gentleman, obviously an Englishman, approached, with the evident intention of reminding the Beauty of the night of her engagement to him, and claiming her, as it were, in the lion's jaws. He advanced a foot, withdrew it, advanced, withdrew; eager for his prize, not over-enterprising; in awe of the illustrious General she entertained—presumeably quite unaware of the pretender's presence; whereupon a voice was heard: 'Oh! if it was minuetting you meant before the lady, I'd never have disputed your right to perform, sir.' For it seemed that there were two claimants in the field, an Irishman and an Englishman; and the former, having a livelier sense of the situation, hung aloof in waiting for her eye; the latter directed himself to strike bluntly at his prey; and he continued minuetting, now rapidly blinking, flushed, angry, conscious of awkwardness and a tangle, incapable of extrication. He began to blink horribly under the raillery of his rival. The General observed him, but as an object remote and minute, a fly or gnat. The face of the brilliant Diana was entirely devoted to him she amused.

Lady Dunstane had the faint lines of a decorous laugh on her lips, as she said: 'How odd it is that our men show to such disadvantage in a Ball- room. I have seen them in danger, and there they shine first of any, and one is proud of them. They should always be facing the elements or in action.' She glanced at the minuet, which had become a petrified figure, still palpitating, bent forward, an interrogative reminder.

Mr. Redworth reserved his assent to the proclamation of any English disadvantage. A whiff of Celtic hostility in the atmosphere put him on his mettle. 'Wherever the man is tried,' he said.

'My lady!' the Irish gentleman bowed to Lady Dunstane. 'I had the honour . . . Sullivan Smith . . . at the castle . . .'

She responded to the salute, and Mr. Sullivan Smith proceeded to tell her, half in speech, half in dots most luminous, of a civil contention between the English gentleman and himself, as to the possession of the loveliest of partners for this particular ensuing dance, and that they had simultaneously made a rush from the Lower Courts, namely, their cards, to the Upper, being the lady; and Mr. Sullivan Smith partly founded his preferable claim on her Irish descent, and on his acquaintance with her eminent defunct father—one of the ever-radiating stars of his quenchless country.

Lady Dunstane sympathized with him for his not intruding his claim when the young lady stood pre-engaged, as well as in humorous appreciation of his imaginative logic.

'There will be dancing enough after supper,' she said.

'If I could score one dance with her, I'd go home supperless and feasted,' said he. 'And that's not saying much among the hordes of hungry troopers tip-toe for the signal to the buffet. See, my lady, the gentleman, as we call him; there he is working his gamut perpetually up to da capo. Oh! but it's a sheep trying to be wolf; he 's sheep-eyed and he 's wolf-fanged, pathetic and larcenous! Oh, now! who'd believe it!— the man has dared . . . I'd as soon think of committing sacrilege in a cathedral!'

The man was actually; to quote his indignant rival, 'breaching the fortress,' and pointing out to Diana Merion 'her name on his dirty scrap of paper': a shocking sight when the lady's recollection was the sole point to be aimed at, and the only umpire. 'As if all of us couldn't have written that, and hadn't done it!' Mr. Sullivan Smith groaned disgusted. He hated bad manners, particularly in cases involving ladies; and the bad manners of a Saxon fired his antagonism to the race; individual members of which he boasted of forgiving and embracing, honouring. So the man blackened the race for him, and the race was excused in the man. But his hatred of bad manners was vehement, and would have extended to a fellow-countryman. His own were of the antecedent century, therefore venerable.

Diana turned from her pursuer with a comic woeful lifting of the brows at her friend. Lady Dunstane motioned her fan, and Diana came, bending head.

'Are you bound in honour?'

'I don't think I am. And I do want to go on talking with the General. He is so delightful and modest—my dream of a true soldier!—telling me of his last big battle, bit by bit, to my fishing.'

'Put off this person for a square dance down the list, and take out Mr. Redworth—Miss Diana Merlon, Mr. Redworth: he will bring you back to the General, who must not totally absorb you, or he will forfeit his popularity.'

Diana instantly struck a treaty with the pertinacious advocate of his claims, to whom, on his relinquishing her, Mr. Sullivan Smith remarked: 'Oh! sir, the law of it, where a lady's concerned! You're one for evictions, I should guess, and the anti-human process. It's that letter of the law that stands between you and me and mine and yours. But you've got your congee, and my blessing on ye!'

'It was a positive engagement,' said the enemy.

Mr. Sullivan Smith derided him. 'And a pretty partner you've pickled for yourself when she keeps her positive engagement!'

He besought Lady Dunstane to console him with a turn. She pleaded weariness. He proposed to sit beside her and divert her. She smiled, but warned him that she was English in every vein. He interjected: 'Irish men and English women! though it's putting the cart before the horse—the copper pennies where the gold guineas should be. So here's the gentleman who takes the oyster, like the lawyer of the fable. English is he? But we read, the last shall be first. And English women and Irish men make the finest coupling in the universe.'

'Well, you must submit to see an Irish woman led out by an English man,' said Lady Dunstane, at the same time informing the obedient Diana, then bestowing her hand on Mr. Redworth to please her friend, that he was a schoolfellow of her husband's.

'Favour can't help coming by rotation, except in very extraordinary circumstances, and he was ahead of me with you, and takes my due, and 'twould be hard on me if I weren't thoroughly indemnified.' Mr. Sullivan Smith bowed. 'You gave them just the start over the frozen minute for conversation; they were total strangers, and he doesn't appear a bad sort of fellow for a temporary mate, though he's not perfectly sure of his legs. And that we'll excuse to any man leading out such a fresh young beauty of a Bright Eyes—like the stars of a winter's night in the frosty season over Columkill, or where you will, so that's in Ireland, to be sure of the likeness to her.'

'Her mother was half English.'

'Of course she was. And what was my observation about the coupling? Dan Merion would make her Irish all over. And she has a vein of Spanish blood in her; for he had; and she's got the colour.— But you spoke of their coupling—or I did. Oh, a man can hold his own with an English roly-poly mate: he's not stifled! But a woman hasn't his power of resistance to dead weight. She's volatile, she's frivolous, a rattler and gabbler—haven't I heard what they say of Irish girls over there? She marries, and it's the end of her sparkling. She must choose at home for a perfect harmonious partner.'

Lady Dunstane expressed her opinion that her couple danced excellently together.

'It'd be a bitter thing to see, if the fellow couldn't dance, after leading her out!' sighed Mr. Sullivan Smith. 'I heard of her over there. They call her the Black Pearl, and the Irish Lily—because she's dark. They rack their poor brains to get the laugh of us.'

'And I listen to you,' said Lady Dunstane.

'Ah! if all England, half, a quarter, the smallest piece of the land were like you, my lady, I'd be loyal to the finger-nails. Now, is she engaged?—when I get a word with her?'

'She is nineteen, or nearly, and she ought to have five good years of freedom, I think.'

'And five good years of serfdom I'd serve to win her!'

A look at him under the eyelids assured Lady Dunstane that there would be small chance for Mr. Sullivan Smith; after a life of bondage, if she knew her Diana, in spite of his tongue, his tact, his lively features, and breadth of shoulders.

Up he sprang. Diana was on Mr. Redworth's arm. 'No refreshments,' she said; and 'this is my refreshment,' taking the seat of Mr. Sullivan Smith, who ejaculated,

'I must go and have that gentleman's name.' He wanted a foe.

'You know you are ready to coquette with the General at any moment, Tony,' said her friend.

'Yes, with the General!'

'He is a noble old man.'

'Superb. And don't say "old man." With his uniform and his height and his grey head, he is like a glorious October day just before the brown leaves fall.'

Diana hummed a little of the air of Planxty Kelly, the favourite of her childhood, as Lady Dunstane well remembered, they smiled together at the scenes and times it recalled.

'Do you still write verses, Tony?'

'I could about him. At one part of the fight he thought he would be beaten. He was overmatched in artillery, and it was a cavalry charge he thundered on them, riding across the field to give the word of command to the couple of regiments, riddled to threads, that gained the day. That is life—when we dare death to live! I wonder at men, who are men, being anything but soldiers! I told you, madre, my own Emmy, I forgave you for marrying, because it was a soldier.'

'Perhaps a soldier is to be the happy man. But you have not told me a word of yourself. What has been done with the old Crossways?'

'The house, you know, is mine. And it's all I have: ten acres and the house, furnished, and let for less than two hundred a year. Oh! how I long to evict the tenants! They can't have my feeling for the place where I was born. They're people of tolerably good connections, middling wealthy, I suppose, of the name of Warwick, and, as far as I can understand, they stick there to be near the Sussex Downs, for a nephew, who likes to ride on them. I've a half engagement, barely legible, to visit them on an indefinite day, and can't bear the idea of strangers masters in the old house. I must be driven there for shelter, for a roof, some month. And I could make a pilgrimage in rain or snow just to doat on the outside of it. That's your Tony.'

'She's my darling.'

'I hear myself speak! But your voice or mine, madre, it's one soul. Be sure I am giving up the ghost when I cease to be one soul with you, dear and dearest! No secrets, never a shadow of a deception, or else I shall feel I am not fit to live. Was I a bad correspondent when you were in India?'

'Pretty well. Copious letters when you did write.'

'I was shy. I knew I should be writing, to Emmy and another, and only when I came to the flow could I forget him. He is very finely built; and I dare say he has a head. I read of his deeds in India and quivered. But he was just a bit in the way. Men are the barriers to perfect naturalness, at least, with girls, I think. You wrote to me in the same tone as ever, and at first I had a struggle to reply. And I, who have such pride in being always myself!'

Two staring semi-circles had formed, one to front the Hero; the other the Beauty. These half moons imperceptibly dissolved to replenish, and became a fixed obstruction.

'Yes, they look,' Diana made answer to Lady Dunstane's comment on the curious impertinence. She was getting used to it, and her friend had a gratification in seeing how little this affected her perfect naturalness.

'You are often in the world—dinners, dances?' she said.

'People are kind.'

'Any proposals?'

'Nibbles.'

'Quite heart-free?'

'Absolutely.'

Diana's unshadowed bright face defied all menace of an eclipse.

The block of sturdy gazers began to melt. The General had dispersed his group of satellites by a movement with the Mayoress on his arm, construed as the signal for procession to the supper-table.

CHAPTER III.
THE INTERIOR OF MR. REDWORTH, AND THE EXTERIOR OF MR. SULLIVAN SMITH

'It may be as well to take Mr. Redworth's arm; you will escape the crush for you,' said Lady Dunstane to Diana. 'I don't sup. Yes! go! You must eat, and he is handiest to conduct you.'

Diana thought of her chaperon and the lateness of the hour. She murmured, to soften her conscience, 'Poor Mrs. Pettigrew!'

And once more Mr. Redworth, outwardly imperturbable, was in the maelstrom of a happiness resembling tempest. He talked, and knew not what he uttered. To give this matchless girl the best to eat and drink was his business, and he performed it. Oddly, for a man who had no loaded design, marshalling the troops in his active and capacious cranium, he fell upon calculations of his income, present and prospective, while she sat at the table and he stood behind her. Others were wrangling for places, chairs, plates, glasses, game-pie, champagne: she had them; the lady under his charge to a certainty would have them; so far good; and he had seven hundred pounds per annum—seven hundred and fifty, in a favourable aspect, at a stretch ....

'Yes, the pleasantest thing to me after working all day is an opera of Carini's,' she said, in full accord with her taste, 'and Tellio for tenor, certainly.'

—A fair enough sum for a bachelor: four hundred personal income, and a prospect of higher dividends to increase it; three hundred odd from his office, and no immediate prospects of an increase there; no one died there, no elderly martyr for the advancement of his juniors could be persuaded to die; they were too tough to think of retiring. Say, seven hundred and fifty .... eight hundred, if the commerce of the country fortified the Bank his property was embarked in; or eight-fifty or nine ten. ...

'I could call him my poet also,' Mr. Redworth agreed with her taste in poets. 'His letters are among the best ever written—or ever published: the raciest English I know. Frank, straight out: capital descriptions. The best English letter-writers are as good as the French—

You don't think so?—in their way, of course. I dare' say we don't sufficiently cultivate the art. We require the supple tongue a closer intercourse of society gives.'

—Eight or ten hundred. Comfortable enough for a man in chambers. To dream of entering as a householder on that sum, in these days, would be stark nonsense: and a man two removes from a baronetcy has no right to set his reckoning on deaths:—if he does, he becomes a sort of meditative assassin. But what were the Fates about when they planted a man of the ability of Tom Redworth in a Government office! Clearly they intended him to remain a bachelor for life. And they sent him over to Ireland on inspection duty for a month to have sight of an Irish Beauty . . . .

'Think war the finest subject for poets?' he exclaimed. 'Flatly no: I don't think it. I think exactly the reverse. It brings out the noblest traits in human character? I won't own that even. It brings out some but under excitement, when you have not always the real man.—Pray don't sneer at domestic life. Well, there was a suspicion of disdain.—Yes, I can respect the hero, military or civil; with this distinction, that the military hero aims at personal reward—'

'He braves wounds and death,' interposed Diana.

'Whereas the civilian hero—'

'Pardon me, let me deny that the soldier-hero aims at a personal reward,' she again interposed.

'He gets it.'

'If he is not beaten.'

'And then he is no longer a hero.'

'He is to me.'

She had a woman's inveterate admiration of the profession of aims. Mr. Redworth endeavoured to render practicable an opening in her mind to reason. He admitted the grandeur of the poetry of Homer. We are a few centuries in advance of Homer. We do not slay damsels for a sacrifice to propitiate celestial wrath; nor do we revel in details of slaughter. He reasoned with her; he repeated stories known to him of civilian heroes, and won her assent to the heroical title for their deeds, but it was languid, or not so bright as the deeds deserved—or as the young lady could look; and he insisted on the civilian hero, impelled by some unconscious motive to make her see the thing he thought, also the thing he was—his plain mind and matter-of-fact nature. Possibly she caught a glimpse of that. After a turn of fencing, in which he was impressed by the vibration of her tones when speaking of military heroes, she quitted the table, saying: 'An argument between one at supper and another handing plates, is rather unequal if eloquence is needed. As Pat said to the constable, when his hands were tied, You beat me with the fists, but my spirit is towering and kicks freely.'

—Eight hundred? a thousand a year, two thousand, are as nothing in the calculation of a householder who means that the mistress of the house shall have the choicest of the fruits and flowers of the Four Quarters; and Thomas Redworth had vowed at his first outlook on the world of women, that never should one of the sisterhood coming under his charge complain of not having them in profusion. Consequently he was a settled bachelor. In the character of disengaged and unaspiring philosophical bachelor, he reviewed the revelations of her character betrayed by the beautiful virgin devoted to the sanguine coat. The thrill of her voice in speaking of soldier-heroes shot him to the yonder side of a gulf. Not knowing why, for he had no scheme, desperate or other, in his head, the least affrighted of men was frightened by her tastes, and by her aplomb, her inoffensiveness in freedom of manner and self-sufficiency—sign of purest breeding: and by her easy, peerless vivacity, her proofs of descent from the blood of Dan Merion—a wildish blood. The candour of the look of her eyes in speaking, her power of looking forthright at men, and looking the thing she spoke, and the play of her voluble lips, the significant repose of her lips in silence, her weighing of the words he uttered, for a moment before the prompt apposite reply, down to her simple quotation of Pat, alarmed him; he did not ask himself why. His manly self was not intruded on his cogitations. A mere eight hundred or thousand per annum had no place in that midst. He beheld her quietly selecting the position of dignity to suit her: an eminent military man, or statesman, or wealthy nobleman: she had but to choose. A war would offer her the decorated soldier she wanted. A war! Such are women of this kind! The thought revolted him, and pricked his appetite for supper. He did service by Mrs. Pettigrew, to which lady Miss Merion, as she said, promoted him, at the table, and then began to refresh in person, standing.

'Malkin! that's the fellow's name' he heard close at his ear.

Mr. Sullivan Smith had drained a champagne-glass, bottle in hand, and was priming the successor to it. He cocked his eye at Mr. Redworth's quick stare. 'Malkin!' And now we'll see whether the interior of him is grey, or black, or tabby, or tortoise-shell, or any other colour of the Malkin breed.'

He explained to Mr. Redworth that he had summoned Mr. Malkin to answer to him as a gentleman for calling Miss Merion a jilt. 'The man, sir, said in my hearing, she jilted him, and that's to call the lady a jilt. There's not a point of difference, not a shade. I overheard him. I happened by the blessing of Providence to be by when he named her publicly jilt. And it's enough that she's a lady to have me for her champion. The same if she had been an Esquimaux squaw. I'll never live to hear a lady insulted.'

'You don't mean to say you're the donkey to provoke a duel!' Mr. Redworth burst out gruffly, through turkey and stuffing.

'And an Irish lady, the young Beauty of Erin!' Mr. Sullivan Smith was flowing on. He became frigid, he politely bowed: 'Two, sir, if you haven't the grace to withdraw the offensive term before it cools and can't be obliterated.'

'Fiddle! and go to the deuce!' Mr. Redworth cried.

'Would a soft slap o' the cheek persuade you, sir?'

'Try it outside, and don't bother me with nonsense of that sort at my supper. If I'm struck, I strike back. I keep my pistols for bandits and law-breakers. Here,' said Mr. Redworth, better inspired as to the way of treating an ultra of the isle; 'touch glasses: you're a gentleman, and won't disturb good company. By-and-by.'

The pleasing prospect of by-and-by renewed in Mr. Sullivan Smith his composure. They touched the foaming glasses: upon which, in a friendly manner, Mr. Sullivan Smith proposed that they should go outside as soon as Mr. Redworth had finished supper-quite finished supper: for the reason that the term 'donkey' affixed to him was like a minster cap of schooldays, ringing bells on his topknot, and also that it stuck in his gizzard.

Mr. Redworth declared the term to be simply hypothetical. 'If you fight, you're a donkey for doing it. But you won't fight.'

'But I will fight.'

'He won't fight.'

'Then for the honour of your country you must. But I'd rather have him first, for I haven't drunk with him, and it should be a case of necessity to put a bullet or a couple of inches of steel through the man you've drunk with. And what's in your favour, she danced with ye. She seemed to take to ye, and the man she has the smallest sugar-melting for is sacred if he's not sweet to me. If he retracts!'

'Hypothetically, No.'

'But supposititiously?'

'Certainly.'

'Then we grasp hands on it. It's Malkin or nothing!' said Mr. Sullivan Smith, swinging his heel moodily to wander in search of the foe. How one sane man could name another a donkey for fighting to clear an innocent young lady's reputation, passed his rational conception.

Sir Lukin hastened to Mr. Redworth to have a talk over old schooldays and fellows.

'I'll tell you what,' said the civilian, 'There are Irishmen and Irishmen. I've met cool heads and long heads among them, and you and I knew Jack Derry, who was good at most things. But the burlesque Irishman can't be caricatured. Nature strained herself in a 'fit of absurdity to produce him, and all that Art can do is to copy.'

This was his prelude to an account of Mr. Sullivan Smith, whom, as a specimen, he rejoiced to have met.

'There's a chance of mischief,' said Sir Lukin. 'I know nothing of the man he calls Malkin. I'll inquire presently.'

He talked of his prospects, and of the women. Fair ones, in his opinion, besides Miss Merion were parading; he sketched two or three of his partners with a broad brush of epithets.

'It won't do for Miss Merion's name to be mixed up in a duel,' said Redworth.

'Not if she's to make her fortune in England,' said Sir Lukin. 'It's probably all smoke.'

The remark had hardly escaped him when a wreath of metaphorical smoke, and fire, and no mean report, startled the company of supping gentlemen. At the pitch of his voice, Mr. Sullivan Smith denounced Mr. Malkin in presence for a cur masquerading as a cat.

'And that is not the scoundrel's prime offence. For what d' ye think? He trumps up an engagement to dance with a beautiful lady, and because she can't remember, binds her to an oath for a dance to come, and then, holding her prisoner to 'm, he sulks, the dirty dogcat goes and sulks, and he won't dance and won't do anything but screech up in corners that he's jilted. He said the word. Dozens of gentlemen heard the word. And I demand an apology of Misterr Malkin—or . . ! And none of your guerrier nodding and bravado, Mister Malkin, at me, if you please. The case is for settlement between gentlemen.'

The harassed gentleman of the name of Malkin, driven to extremity by the worrying, stood in braced preparation for the English attitude of defence. His tormentor drew closer to him.

'Mind, I give you warning, if you lay a finger on me I'll knock you down,' said he.

Most joyfully Mr. Sullivan Smith uttered a low melodious cry. 'For a specimen of manners, in an assembly of ladies and gentlemen . . . I ask ye!' he addressed the ring about him, to put his adversary entirely in the wrong before provoking the act of war. And then, as one intending gently to remonstrate, he was on the point of stretching out his finger to the shoulder of Mr. Malkin, when Redworth seized his arm, saying: 'I 'm your man: me first: you're due to me.'

Mr. Sullivan Smith beheld the vanishing of his foe in a cloud of faces. Now was he wroth on patently reasonable grounds. He threatened Saxondom. Man up, man down, he challenged the race of short-legged, thickset, wooden-gated curmudgeons: and let it be pugilism if their white livers shivered at the notion of powder and ball. Redworth, in the struggle to haul him away, received a blow from him. 'And you've got it! you would have it!' roared the Celt.

'Excuse yourself to the company for a misdirected effort,' Redworth said; and he observed generally: 'No Irish gentleman strikes a blow in good company.'

'But that's true as Writ! And I offer excuses—if you'll come along with me and a couple of friends. The thing has been done before by torchlight—and neatly.'

'Come along, and come alone,' said Redworth.

A way was cleared for them. Sir Lukin hurried up to Redworth, who had no doubt of his ability to manage Mr. Sullivan Smith.

He managed that fine-hearted but purely sensational fellow so well that Lady Dunstane and Diana, after hearing in some anxiety of the hubbub below, beheld them entering the long saloon amicably, with the nods and looks of gentlemen quietly accordant.

A little later, Lady Dunstane questioned Redworth, and he smoothed her apprehensions, delivering himself, much to her comfort, thus: 'In no case would any lady's name have been raised. The whole affair was nonsensical. He's a capital fellow of a kind, capable of behaving like a man of the world and a gentleman. Only he has, or thinks he has, like lots of his countrymen, a raw wound—something that itches to be grazed. Champagne on that! . . . Irishmen, as far as I have seen of them, are, like horses, bundles of nerves; and you must manage them, as you do with all nervous creatures, with firmness, but good temper. You must never get into a fury of the nerves yourself with them. Spur and whip they don't want; they'll be off with you in a jiffy if you try it.

They want the bridle-rein. That seems to me the secret of Irish character. We English are not bad horsemen. It's a wonder we blunder so in our management of such a people.'

'I wish you were in a position to put your method to the proof,' said she.

He shrugged. 'There's little chance of it!'

To reward him for his practical discretion, she contrived that Diana should give him a final dance; and the beautiful gill smiled quickly responsive to his appeal. He was, moreover, sensible in her look and speech that he had advanced in her consideration to be no longer the mere spinning stick, a young lady's partner. By which he humbly understood that her friend approved him. A gentle delirium enfolded his brain. A householder's life is often begun on eight hundred a year: on less: on much less:—sometimes on nothing but resolution to make a fitting income, carving out a fortune. Eight hundred may stand as a superior basis. That sum is a distinct point of vantage. If it does not mean a carriage and Parisian millinery and a station for one of the stars of society, it means at any rate security; and then, the heart of the man being strong and sound . . .

'Yes,' he replied to her, 'I like my experience of Ireland and the Irish; and better than I thought I should. St. George's Channel ought to be crossed oftener by both of us.'

'I'm always glad of the signal,' said Diana.

He had implied the people of the two islands. He allowed her interpretation to remain personal, for the sake of a creeping deliciousness that it carried through his blood.

'Shall you soon be returning to England?' he ventured to ask.—

'I am Lady Dunstane's guest for some months.'

'Then you will. Sir Lukin has an estate in Surrey. He talks of quitting the Service.'

'I can't believe it!'

His thrilled blood was chilled. She entertained a sentiment amounting to adoration for the profession of arms!

Gallantly had the veteran General and Hero held on into the night, that the festivity might not be dashed by his departure; perhaps, to a certain degree, to prolong his enjoyment of a flattering scene. At last Sir Lukin had the word from him, and came to his wife. Diana slipped across the floor to her accommodating chaperon, whom, for the sake of another five minutes with her beloved Emma, she very agreeably persuaded to walk in the train of Lord Larrian, and forth they trooped down

a pathway of nodding heads and curtsies, resembling oak and birch-trees under a tempered gale, even to the shedding of leaves, for here a turban was picked up by Sir Lukin, there a jewelled ear-ring by the self- constituted attendant, Mr. Thomas Redworth. At the portico rang a wakening cheer, really worth hearing. The rain it rained, and hats were formless,' as in the first conception of the edifice, backs were damp, boots liquidly musical, the pipe of consolation smoked with difficulty, with much pulling at the stem, but the cheer arose magnificently, and multiplied itself, touching at the same moment the heavens and Diana's heart-at least, drawing them together; for she felt exalted, enraptured, as proud of her countrymen as of their hero.

'That's the natural shamrock, after the artificial!' she heard Mr. Redworth say, behind her.

She turned and sent one of her brilliant glances flying over him, in gratitude for a timely word well said. And she never forgot the remark, nor he the look.

CHAPTER IV.
CONTAINING HINTS OF DIANA'S EXPERIENCES AND OF WHAT THEY LED TO

A fortnight after this memorable Ball the principal actors of both sexes had crossed the Channel back to England, and old Ireland was left to her rains from above and her undrained bogs below; her physical and her mental vapours; her ailments and her bog-bred doctors; as to whom the governing country trusted they would be silent or discourse humorously.

The residence of Sir Lukin Dunstane, in the county of Surrey, inherited by him during his recent term of Indian services, was on the hills, where a day of Italian sky, or better, a day of our breezy South-west, washed from the showery night, gives distantly a tower to view, and a murky web, not without colour: the ever-flying banner of the metropolis, the smoke of the city's chimneys, if you prefer plain language. At a first inspection of the house, Lady Dunstane did not like it, and it was advertized to be let, and the auctioneer proclaimed it in his dialect. Her taste was delicate; she had the sensitiveness of an invalid: twice she read the stalking advertizement of the attractions of Copsley, and hearing Diana call it 'the plush of speech,' she shuddered; she decided that a place where her husband's family had lived ought not to stand forth meretriciously spangled and daubed, like a show-booth at a fair, for a bait; though the grandiloquent man of advertizing letters assured Sir Lukin that a public agape for the big and gaudy mouthful is in no milder way to be caught; as it is apparently the case. She withdrew the trumpeting placard. Retract we likewise 'banner of the metropolis.' That plush of speech haunts all efforts to swell and illuminate citizen prose to a princely poetic.

Yet Lady Dunstane herself could name the bank of smoke, when looking North-eastward from her summerhouse, the flag of London: and she was a person of the critical mind, well able to distinguish between the simple metaphor and the superobese. A year of habitation induced her to conceal her dislike of the place in love: cat's love, she owned. Here, she confessed to Diana, she would wish to live to her end. It seemed remote, where an invigorating upper air gave new bloom to her cheeks; but she kept one secret from her friend.

Copsley was an estate of nearly twelve hundred acres, extending across the ridge of the hills to the slopes North and South. Seven counties rolled their backs under this commanding height, and it would have tasked a pigeon to fly within an hour the stretch of country visible at the Copsley windows. Sunrise to right, sunset leftward, the borders of the grounds held both flaming horizons. So much of the heavens and of earth is rarely granted to a dwelling. The drawback was the structure, which had no charm, scarce a face. 'It is written that I should live in barracks,' Lady Dunstane said. The colour of it taught white to impose a sense of gloom. Her cat's love of the familiar inside corners was never able to embrace the outer walls. Her sensitiveness, too, was racked by the presentation of so pitiably ugly a figure to the landscape. She likened it to a coarse-featured country wench, whose cleaning and decorating of her countenance makes complexion grin and ruggedness yawn. Dirty, dilapidated, hung with weeds and parasites, it would have been more tolerable. She tried the effect of various creepers, and they were as a staring paint. What it was like then, she had no heart to say.

One may, however, fall on a pleasurable resignation in accepting great indemnities, as Diana bade her believe, when the first disgust began to ebb. 'A good hundred over there would think it a Paradise for an asylum': she signified London. Her friend bore such reminders meekly. They were readers of books of all sorts, political, philosophical, economical, romantic; and they mixed the diverse readings in thought, after the fashion of the ardently youthful. Romance affected politics, transformed economy, irradiated philosophy. They discussed the knotty question, Why things were not done, the things being confessedly to do; and they cut the knot: Men, men calling themselves statesmen, declined to perform that operation, because, forsooth, other men objected to have it performed on them. And common humanity declared it to be for the common weal! If so, then it is clearly indicated as a course of action: we shut our eyes against logic and the vaunted laws of economy. They are the knot we cut; or would cut, had we the sword. Diana did it to the tune of Garryowen or Planxty Kelly. O for a despot! The cry was for a beneficent despot, naturally: a large-minded benevolent despot. In short, a despot to obey their bidding. Thoughtful young people who think through the heart soon come to this conclusion. The heart is the beneficent despot they would be. He cures those miseries; he creates the novel harmony. He sees all difficulties through his own sanguine hues. He is the musical poet of the problem, demanding merely to have it solved that he may sing: clear proof of the necessity for solving it immediately.

Thus far in their pursuit of methods for the government of a nation, to make it happy, Diana was leader. Her fine ardour and resonance, and more than the convincing ring of her voice, the girl's impassioned rapidity in rushing through any perceptible avenue of the labyrinth, or beating down obstacles to form one, and coming swiftly to some solution, constituted her the chief of the pair of democratic rebels in questions that clamoured for instant solution. By dint of reading solid writers, using the brains they possessed, it was revealed to them gradually that their particular impatience came perhaps of the most earnest desire to get to a comfortable termination of the inquiry: the heart aching for mankind sought a nest for itself. At this point Lady Dunstane took the lead. Diana had to be tugged to follow. She could not accept a 'perhaps' that cast dubiousness on her disinterested championship. She protested a perfect certainty of the single aim of her heart outward. But she reflected. She discovered that her friend had gone ahead of her.

The discovery was reached, and even acknowledged, before she could persuade herself to swallow the repulsive truth. O self! self! self! are we eternally masking in a domino that reveals your hideous old face when we could be most positive we had escaped you? Eternally! the desolating answer knelled. Nevertheless the poor, the starving, the overtaxed in labour, they have a right to the cry of Now! now! They have; and if a cry could conduct us to the secret of aiding, healing, feeding, elevating them, we might swell the cry. As it is, we must lay it on our wits patiently to track and find the secret; and meantime do what the individual with his poor pittance can. A miserable contribution! sighed the girl. Old Self was perceived in the sigh. She was haunted.

After all, one must live one's life. Placing her on a lower pedestal in her self-esteem, the philosophy of youth revived her; and if the abatement of her personal pride was dispiriting, she began to see an advantage in getting inward eyes.

'It's infinitely better I should know it, Emmy—I'm a reptile! Pleasure here, pleasure there, I'm always thinking of pleasure. I shall give up thinking and take to drifting. Neither of us can do more than open purses; and mine's lean. If the old Crossways had no tenant, it would be a purse all mouth. And charity is haunted, like everything we do. Only I say with my whole strength yes, I am sure, in spite of the men professing that they are practical, the rich will not move without a goad. I have and hold—you shall hunger and covet, until you are strong enough to force my hand:—that's the speech of the wealthy. And they are Christians. In name. Well, I thank heaven I'm at war, with myself.'

'You always manage to strike out a sentence worth remembering, Tony,' said Lady Dunstane. 'At war with ourselves, means the best happiness we can have.'

It suited her, frail as her health was, and her wisdom striving to the spiritual of happiness. War with herself was far from happiness in the bosom of Diana. She wanted external life, action, fields for energies, to vary the struggle. It fretted and rendered her ill at ease. In her solitary rides with Sir Lukin through a long winter season, she appalled that excellent but conventionally-minded gentleman by starting, nay supporting, theories next to profane in the consideration of a land-owner. She spoke of Reform: of the Repeal of the Corn Laws as the simple beginning of the grants due to the people. She had her ideas, of course, from that fellow Redworth, an occasional visitor at Copsley; and a man might be a donkey and think what he pleased, since he had a vocabulary to back his opinions. A woman, Sir Lukin held, was by nature a mute in politics. Of the thing called a Radical woman, he could not believe that she was less than monstrous: 'with a nose,' he said; and doubtless, horse teeth, hatchet jaws, slatternly in the gown, slipshod, awful. As for a girl, an unmarried, handsome girl, admittedly beautiful, her interjections, echoing a man, were ridiculous, and not a little annoying now and them, for she could be piercingly sarcastic. Her vocabulary in irony was a quiverful. He admired her and liked her immensely; complaining only of her turn for unfeminine topics. He pardoned her on the score of the petty difference rankling between them in reference to his abandonment of his Profession, for here she was patriotically wrong-headed. Everybody knew that he had sold out in order to look after his estates of Copsley and Dunena, secondly: and in the first place, to nurse and be a companion to his wife. He had left her but four times in five months; he had spent just three weeks of that time away from her in London. No one could doubt of his having kept his pledge, although his wife occupied herself with books and notions and subjects foreign to his taste—his understanding, too, he owned. And Redworth had approved of his retirement, had a contempt for soldiering. 'Quite as great as yours for civilians, I can tell you,' Sir Lukin said, dashing out of politics to the vexatious personal subject. Her unexpressed disdain was ruffling.

'Mr. Redworth recommends work: he respects the working soldier,' said Diana.

Sir Lukin exclaimed that he had been a working soldier; he was ready to serve if his country wanted him. He directed her to anathematize Peace, instead of scorning a fellow for doing the duties next about him: and the mention of Peace fetched him at a bound back to politics. He quoted a distinguished Tory orator, to the effect, that any lengthened term of peace bred maggots in the heads of the people.

'Mr. Redworth spoke of it: he translated something from Aristophanes for a retort,' said Diana.

'Well, we're friends, eh?' Sir Lukin put forth a hand.

She looked at him surprised at the unnecessary call for a show, of friendship; she touched his hand with two tips of her fingers, remarking, 'I should think so, indeed.'

He deemed it prudent to hint to his wife that Diana Merion appeared to be meditating upon Mr. Redworth.

'That is a serious misfortune, if true,' said Lady Dunstane. She thought so for two reasons: Mr. Redworth generally disagreed in opinion with Diana, and contradicted her so flatly as to produce the impression of his not even sharing the popular admiration of her beauty; and, further, she hoped for Diana to make a splendid marriage. The nibbles threatened to be snaps and bites. There had been a proposal, in an epistle, a quaint effusion, from a gentleman avowing that he had seen her, and had not danced with her on the night of the Irish ball. He was rejected, but Diana groaned over the task of replying to the unfortunate applicant, so as not to wound him. 'Shall I have to do this often, I wonder?' she said.

'Unless you capitulate,' said her friend.

Diana's exclamation: 'May I be heart-free for another ten years!' encouraged Lady Dunstane to suppose her husband quite mistaken.

In the Spring Diana, went on a first pilgrimage to her old home, The Crossways, and was kindly entertained by the uncle and aunt of a treasured nephew, Mr. Augustus Warwick. She rode with him on the Downs. A visit of a week humanized her view of the intruders. She wrote almost tenderly of her host and hostess to Lady Dunstane; they had but 'the one fault—of spoiling their nephew.' Him she described as a 'gentlemanly official,' a picture of him. His age was thirty-four. He seemed 'fond of her scenery.' Then her pen swept over the Downs like a flying horse. Lady Dunstane thought no more of the gentlemanly official. He was a barrister who did not practise: in nothing the man for Diana. Letters came from the house of the Pettigrews in Kent; from London; from Halford Manor in Hertfordshire; from Lockton Grange in Lincolnshire: after which they ceased to be the thrice weekly; and reading the latest of them, Lady Dunstane imagined a flustered quill. The letter succeeding the omission contained no excuse, and it was brief. There was a strange interjection, as to the wearifulness of constantly wandering, like a leaf off the tree. Diana spoke of looking for a return of the dear winter days at Copsley. That was her station. Either she must have had some disturbing experience, or Copsley was dear for a Redworth reason, thought the anxious peruser; musing, dreaming, putting together divers shreds of correspondence and testing them with her intimate knowledge of Diana's character, Lady Dunstane conceived that the unprotected beautiful girl had suffered a persecution, it might be an insult. She spelt over the names of the guests at the houses. Lord Wroxeter was of evil report: Captain Rampan, a Turf captain, had the like notoriety. And it is impossible in a great house for the hostess to spread her aegis to cover every dame and damsel present. She has to depend on the women being discreet, the men civilized.

'How brutal men can be!' was one of Diana's incidental remarks, in a subsequent letter, relating simply to masculine habits. In those days the famous ancestral plea of 'the passion for his charmer' had not been altogether socially quashed down among the provinces, where the bottle maintained a sort of sway, and the beauty which inflamed the sons of men was held to be in coy expectation of violent effects upon their boiling blood. There were, one hears that there still are, remnants of the pristine male, who, if resisted in their suing, conclude that they are scorned, and it infuriates them: some also whose 'passion for the charmer' is an instinct to pull down the standard of the sex, by a bully imposition of sheer physical ascendancy, whenever they see it flying with an air of gallant independence: and some who dedicate their lives to a study of the arts of the Lord Of Reptiles, until they have worked the crisis for a display of him in person. Assault or siege, they have achieved their triumphs; they have dominated a frailer system of nerves, and a young woman without father, or brother, or husband, to defend her, is cryingly a weak one, therefore inviting to such an order of heroes. Lady Dunstane was quick-witted and had a talkative husband; she knew a little of the upper social world of her time. She was heartily glad to have Diana by her side again.

Not a word of any serious experience was uttered. Only on one occasion while they conversed, something being mentioned of her tolerance, a flush of swarthy crimson shot over Diana, and she frowned, with the outcry 'Oh! I have discovered that I can be a tigress!'

Her friend pressed her hand, saying, 'The cause a good one!'

'Women have to fight.'

Diana said no more. There had been a bad experience of her isolated position in the world.

Lady Dunstane now indulged a partial hope that Mr. Redworth might see in this unprotected beautiful girl a person worthy of his esteem. He had his opportunities, and evidently he liked her. She appeared to take more cordially to him. She valued the sterling nature of the man. But they were a hopeless couple, they were so friendly. Both ladies noticed in him an abstractedness of look, often when conversing, as of a man in calculation; they put it down to an ambitious mind. Yet Diana said then, and said always, that it was he who had first taught her the art of observing. On the whole, the brilliant marriage seemed a fairer prospect for her; how reasonable to anticipate, Lady Dunstane often thought when admiring the advance of Diana's beauty in queenliness, for never did woman carry her head more grandly, more thrillingly make her presence felt; and if only she had been an actress showing herself nightly on a London stage, she would before now have met the superb appreciation, melancholy to reflect upon!

Diana regained her happy composure at Copsley. She had, as she imagined, no ambition. The dulness of the place conveyed a charm to a nature recovering from disturbance to its clear smooth flow. Air, light, books, and her friend, these good things she had; they were all she wanted. She rode, she walked, with Sir Lukin or Mr. Redworth, for companion; or with Saturday and Sunday guests, Lord Larrian, her declared admirer, among them. 'Twenty years younger!' he said to her, shrugging, with a merry smile drawn a little at the corners to sober sourness; and she vowed to her friend that she would not have had the heart to refuse him. 'Though,' said she, 'speaking generally, I cannot tell you what a foreign animal a husband would appear in my kingdom.' Her experience had wakened a sexual aversion, of some slight kind, enough to make her feminine pride stipulate for perfect independence, that she might have the calm out of which imagination spreads wing. Imagination had become her broader life, and on such an earth, under such skies, a husband who is not the fountain of it, certainly is a foreign animal: he is a discordant note. He contracts the ethereal world, deadens radiancy. He is gross fact, a leash, a muzzle, harness, a hood; whatever is detestable to the free limbs and senses. It amused Lady Dunstane to hear Diana say, one evening when their conversation fell by hazard on her future, that the idea of a convent was more welcome to her than the most splendid marriage. 'For,' she added, 'as I am sure I shall never know anything of this love they rattle about and rave about, I shall do well to keep to my good single path; and I have a warning within me that a step out of it will be a wrong one—for me, dearest!'

She wished her view of the yoke to be considered purely personal, drawn from no examples and comparisons. The excellent Sir Lukin was passing a great deal of his time in London. His wife had not a word of blame for him; he was a respectful husband, and attentive when present; but so uncertain, owing to the sudden pressure of engagements, that Diana, bound on a second visit to The Crossways, doubted whether she would be able to quit her friend, whose condition did not allow of her being left solitary at Copsley. He came nevertheless a day before Diana's appointed departure on her round of visits. She was pleased with him, and let him see it, for the encouragement of a husband in the observance of his duties. One of the horses had fallen lame, so they went out for a walk, at Lady Dunstane's request. It was a delicious afternoon of Spring, with the full red disk of sun dropping behind the brown beech-twigs. She remembered long afterward the sweet simpleness of her feelings as she took in the scent of wild flowers along the lanes and entered the woods jaws of another monstrous and blackening experience. He fell into the sentimental vein, and a man coming from that heated London life to these glorified woods, might be excused for doing so, though it sounded to her just a little ludicrous in him. She played tolerantly second to it; she quoted a snatch of poetry, and his whole face was bent to her, with the petition that she would repeat the verse. Much struck was this giant ex- dragoon. Ah! how fine! grand! He would rather hear that than any opera: it was diviner! 'Yes, the best poetry is,' she assented. 'On your lips,' he said. She laughed. 'I am not a particularly melodious reciter.' He vowed he could listen to her eternally, eternally. His face, on a screw of the neck and shoulders, was now perpetually three- quarters fronting. Ah! she was going to leave. 'Yes, and you will find my return quite early enough,' said Diana, stepping a trifle more briskly. His fist was raised on the length of the arm, as if in invocation. 'Not in the whole of London is there a woman worthy to fasten your shoe-buckles! My oath on it! I look; I can't spy one.' Such was his flattering eloquence.

She told him not to think it necessary to pay her compliments. 'And here, of all places!' They were in the heart of the woods. She found her hand seized—her waist. Even then, so impossible is it to conceive the unimaginable even when the apparition of it smites us, she expected some protesting absurdity, or that he had seen something in her path.— What did she hear? And from her friend's husband!

If stricken idiotic, he was a gentleman; the tigress she had detected in her composition did not require to be called forth; half-a-dozen words, direct, sharp as fangs and teeth, with the eyes burning over them, sufficed for the work of defence. 'The man who swore loyalty to Emma!' Her reproachful repulsion of eyes was unmistakeable, withering; as masterful as a superior force on his muscles.—What thing had he been taking her for?—She asked it within: and he of himself, in a reflective gasp. Those eyes of hers appeared as in a cloud, with the wrath above: she had: the look of a Goddess in anger. He stammered, pleaded across her flying shoulder—Oh! horrible, loathsome, pitiable to hear! . . . 'A momentary aberration . . . her beauty . . . he deserved to be shot! . . . could not help admiring . . . quite lost his head . . on his honour! never again !'

Once in the roadway, and Copsley visible, she checked her arrowy pace for breath, and almost commiserated the dejected wretch in her thankfulness to him for silence. Nothing exonerated him, but at least he had the grace not to beg secresy. That would have been an intolerable whine of a poltroon, adding to her humiliation. He abstained; he stood at her mercy without appealing.

She was not the woman to take poor vengeance. But, Oh! she was profoundly humiliated, shamed through and through. The question, was I guilty of any lightness—anything to bring this on me? would not be laid. And how she pitied her friend! This house, her heart's home, was now a wreck to her: nay, worse, a hostile citadel. The burden of the task of meeting Emma with an open face, crushed her like very guilt. Yet she succeeded. After an hour in her bedchamber she managed to lock up her heart and summon the sprite of acting to her tongue and features: which ready attendant on the suffering female host performed his liveliest throughout the evening, to Emma's amusement, and to the culprit ex- dragoon's astonishment; in whom, to tell the truth of him, her sparkle and fun kindled the sense of his being less criminal than he had supposed, with a dim vision of himself as the real proven donkey for not having been a harmless dash more so. But, to be just as well as penetrating, this was only the effect of her personal charm on his nature. So it spurred him a moment, when it struck this doleful man that to have secured one kiss of those fresh and witty sparkling lips he would endure forfeits, pangs, anything save the hanging of his culprit's head before his Emma. Reflection washed him clean. Secresy is not a medical restorative, by no means a good thing for the baffled amorously- adventurous cavalier, unless the lady's character shall have been firmly established in or over his hazy wagging noddle. Reflection informed him that the honourable, generous, proud girl spared him for the sake of the house she loved. After a night of tossing, he rose right heartily repentant. He showed it in the best manner, not dramatically. On her accepting his offer to drive her down to the valley to meet the coach, a genuine illumination of pure gratitude made a better man of him, both to look at and in feeling. She did not hesitate to consent; and he had half expected a refusal. She talked on the way quite as usual, cheerfully, if not altogether so spiritedly. A flash of her matchless wit now and then reduced him to that abject state of man beside the fair person he has treated high cavalierly, which one craves permission to describe as pulp. He was utterly beaten.

The sight of Redworth on the valley road was a relief to them both. He had slept in one of the houses of the valley, and spoke of having had the intention to mount to Copsley. Sir Lukin proposed to drive him back. He glanced at Diana, still with that calculating abstract air of his; and he was rallied. He confessed to being absorbed in railways, the new lines of railways projected to thread the land and fast mapping it.

'You 've not embarked money in them?' said Sir Lukin.

The answer was: 'I have; all I possess.' And Redworth for a sharp instant set his eyes on Diana, indifferent to Sir Lukin's bellow of stupefaction at such gambling on the part of a prudent fellow.

He asked her where she was to be met, where written to, during the Summer, in case of his wishing to send her news.

She replied: 'Copsley will be the surest. I am always in communication with Lady Dunstane.' She coloured deeply. The recollection of the change of her feeling for Copsley suffused her maiden mind.

The strange blush prompted an impulse in Redworth to speak to her at once of his venture in railways. But what would she understand of them, as connected with the mighty stake he was playing for? He delayed. The coach came at a trot of the horses, admired by Sir Lukin, round a corner. She entered it, her maid followed, the door banged, the horses trotted. She was off.

Her destiny of the Crossways tied a knot, barred a gate, and pointed to a new direction of the road on that fine spring morning, when beech-buds were near the burst, cowslips yellowed the meadow-flats, and skylarks quivered upward.

For many long years Redworth had in his memory, for a comment on procrastination and excessive scrupulousness in his calculating faculty, the blue back of a coach.

He declined the vacated place beside Sir Lukin, promising to come and spend a couple of days at Copsley in a fortnight—Saturday week. He wanted, he said, to have a talk with Lady Dunstane. Evidently he had railways on the brain, and Sir Lukin warned his wife to be guarded against the speculative mania, and advise the man, if she could.

CHAPTER V.
CONCERNING THE SCRUPULOUS GENTLEMAN WHO CAME TOO LATE

On the Saturday of his appointment Redworth arrived at Copsley, with a shade deeper of the calculating look under his thick brows, habitual to him latterly. He found Lady Dunstane at her desk, pen in hand, the paper untouched; and there was an appearance of trouble about her somewhat resembling his own, as he would have observed, had he been open-minded enough to notice anything, except that she was writing a letter. He begged her to continue it; he proposed to read a book till she was at leisure.

'I have to write, and scarcely know how,' said she, clearing her face to make the guest at home, and taking a chair by the fire, 'I would rather chat for half an hour.'

She spoke of the weather, frosty, but tonic; bad for the last days of hunting, good for the farmer and the country, let us hope.

Redworth nodded assent. It might be surmised that he was brooding over those railways, in which he had embarked his fortune. Ah! those railways! She was not long coming to the wailful exclamation upon them, both to express her personal sorrow at the disfigurement of our dear England, and lead to a little, modest, offering of a woman's counsel to the rash adventurer; for thus could she serviceably put aside her perplexity awhile. Those railways! When would there be peace in the land? Where one single nook of shelter and escape from them! And the English, blunt as their senses are to noise and hubbub, would be revelling in hisses, shrieks, puffings and screeches, so that travelling would become an intolerable affliction. 'I speak rather as an invalid,' she admitted; 'I conjure up all sorts of horrors, the whistle in the night beneath one's windows, and the smoke of trains defacing the landscape; hideous accidents too. They will be wholesale and past help. Imagine a collision! I have borne many changes with equanimity, I pretend to a certain degree of philosophy, but this mania for cutting up the land does really cause me to pity those who are to follow us. They will not see the England we have seen. It will be patched and scored, disfigured . . . a sort of barbarous Maori visage—England in a New Zealand mask. You may call it the sentimental view. In this case, I am decidedly sentimental: I love my country. I do love quiet, rural England. Well, and I love beauty, I love simplicity. All that will be destroyed by the refuse of the towns flooding the land—barring accidents, as Lukin says. There seems nothing else to save us.'

Redworth acquiesced. 'Nothing.'

'And you do not regret it?' he was asked.

'Not a bit. We have already exchanged opinions on the subject. Simplicity must go, and the townsman meet his equal in the countryman. As for beauty, I would sacrifice that to circulate gumption. A bushelful of nonsense is talked pro and con: it always is at an innovation. What we are now doing, is to take a longer and a quicker stride, that is all.'

'And establishing a new field for the speculator.'

'Yes, and I am one, and this is the matter I wanted to discuss with you, Lady Dunstane,' said Redworth, bending forward, the whole man devoted to the point of business.

She declared she was complimented; she felt the compliment, and trusted her advice might be useful, faintly remarking that she had a woman's head: and 'not less' was implied as much as 'not more,' in order to give strength to her prospective opposition.

All his money, she heard, was down on the railway table. He might within a year have a tolerable fortune: and, of course, he might be ruined. He did not expect it; still he fronted the risks. 'And now,' said he, 'I come to you for counsel. I am not held among my acquaintances to be a marrying man, as it's called.'

He paused. Lady Dunstane thought it an occasion to praise him for his considerateness.

'You involve no one but yourself, you mean?' Her eyes shed approval. 'Still the day may come . . . I say only that it may: and the wish to marry is a rosy colouring . . . equal to a flying chariot in conducting us across difficulties and obstructions to the deed. And then one may have to regret a previous rashness.'

These practical men are sometimes obtuse: she dwelt on that vision of the future.

He listened, and resumed: 'My view of marriage is, that no man should ask a woman to be his wife unless he is well able to support her in the comforts, not to say luxuries, she is accustomed to.' His gaze had wandered to the desk; it fixed there. 'That is Miss Merion's writing,' he said.

'The letter?' said Lady Dunstane, and she stretched out her hand to press down a leaf of it. 'Yes; it is from her.'

'Is she quite well?'

'I suppose she is. She does not speak of her health.'

He looked pertinaciously in the direction of the letter, and it was not rightly mannered. That letter, of all others, was covert and sacred to the friend. It contained the weightiest of secrets.

'I have not written to her,' said Redworth.

He was astonishing: 'To whom? To Diana? You could very well have done so, only I fancy she knows nothing, has never given a thought to railway stocks and shares; she has a loathing for speculation.'

'And speculators too, I dare say!'

'It is extremely probable.' Lady Dunstane spoke with an emphasis, for the man liked Diana, and would be moved by the idea of forfeiting her esteem.

'She might blame me if I did anything dishonourable!'

'She certainly would.'

'She will have no cause.'

Lady Dunstane began to look, as at a cloud charged with remote explosions: and still for the moment she was unsuspecting. But it was a flitting moment. When he went on, and very singularly droning to her ear: 'The more a man loves a woman, the more he should be positive, before asking her, that she will not have to consent to a loss of position, and I would rather lose her than fail to give her all—not be sure, as far as a man can be sure, of giving her all I think she's worthy of': then the cloud shot a lightning flash, and the doors of her understanding swung wide to the entry of a great wonderment. A shock of pain succeeded it. Her sympathy was roused so acutely that she slipped over the reflective rebuke she would have addressed to her silly delusion concerning his purpose in speaking of his affairs to a woman. Though he did not mention Diana by name, Diana was clearly the person. And why had he delayed to speak to her?—Because of this venture of his money to make him a fortune, for the assurance of her future comfort! Here was the best of men for the girl, not displeasing to her; a good, strong, trustworthy man, pleasant to hear and to see, only erring in being a trifle too scrupulous in love: and a fortnight back she would have imagined he had no chance; and now she knew that the chance was excellent in those days, with this revelation in Diana's letter, which said that all chance was over.

'The courtship of a woman,' he droned away, 'is in my mind not fair to her until a man has to the full enough to sanction his asking her to marry him. And if he throws all he possesses on a stake . . . to win her—give her what she has a right to claim, he ought . . . . Only at present the prospect seems good . . . . He ought of course to wait. Well, the value of the stock I hold has doubled, and it increases. I am a careful watcher of the market. I have friends—brokers and railway Directors. I can rely on them.'

'Pray,' interposed Lady Dunstane, 'specify—I am rather in a mist—the exact point upon which you do me the honour to consult me.' She ridiculed herself for having imagined that such a man would come to consult her upon a point of business.

'It is,' he replied, 'this: whether, as affairs now stand with me—I have an income from my office, and personal property . . . say between thirteen and fourteen hundred a year to start with—whether you think me justified in asking a lady to share my lot?'

'Why not? But will you name the lady?'

'Then I may write at once? In your judgement. . . . Yes, the lady. I have not named her. I had no right. Besides, the general question first, in fairness to the petitioner. You might reasonably stipulate for more for a friend. She could make a match, as you have said . . .' he muttered of 'brilliant,' and 'the highest'; and his humbleness of the honest man enamoured touched Lady Dunstane. She saw him now as the man of strength that she would have selected from a thousand suitors to guide her dear friend.

She caught at a straw: 'Tell me, it is not Diana?'

'Diana Merion!'

As soon as he had said it he perceived pity, and he drew himself tight for the stroke. 'She's in love with some one?'

'She is engaged.'

He bore it well. He was a big-chested fellow, and that excruciating twist within of the revolution of the wheels of the brain snapping their course to grind the contrary to that of the heart, was revealed in one short lift and gasp, a compression of the tremendous change he underwent.

'Why did you not speak before?' said Lady Dunstane. Her words were tremulous.

'I should have had no justification!'

'You might have won her!' She could have wept; her sympathy and her self-condolence under disappointment at Diana's conduct joined to swell the feminine flood.

The poor fellow's quick breathing and blinking reminded her of cruelty in a retrospect. She generalized, to ease her spirit of regret, by hinting it without hurting: 'Women really are not puppets. They are not so excessively luxurious. It is good for young women in the early days of marriage to rough it a little.' She found herself droning, as he had done.

He had ears for nothing but the fact.

'Then I am too late!'

'I have heard it to-day.'

'She is engaged! Positively?'

Lady Dunstane glanced backward at the letter on her desk. She had to answer the strangest of letters that had ever come to her, and it was from her dear Tony, the baldest intimation of the weightiest piece of intelligence which a woman can communicate to her heart's friend. The task of answering it was now doubled. 'I fear so, I fancy so,' she said, and she longed to cast eye over the letter again, to see if there might possibly be a loophole behind the lines.

'Then I must make my mind up to it,' said Redworth. 'I think I'll take a walk.'

She smiled kindly. 'It will be our secret.'

'I thank you with all my heart, Lady Dunstane.'

He was not a weaver of phrases in distress. His blunt reserve was eloquent of it to her, and she liked him the better; could have thanked him, too, for leaving her promptly.

When she was alone she took in the contents of the letter at a hasty glimpse. It was of one paragraph, and fired its shot like a cannon with the muzzle at her breast:—

> 'MY OWN EMMY,—I have been asked in marriage by Mr. Warwick, and have accepted him. Signify your approval, for I have decided that it is the wisest thing a waif can do. We are to live at The Crossways for four months of the year, so I shall have Dada in his best days and all my youngest dreams, my sunrise and morning dew, surrounding me; my old home for my new one. I write in haste, to you first, burning to hear from you. Send your blessing to yours in life and death, through all transformations, 'TONY.'

That was all. Not a word of the lover about to be decorated with the title of husband. No confession of love, nor a single supplicating word to her friend, in excuse for the abrupt decision to so grave a step. Her previous description of, him, as a 'gentlemanly official' in his appearance, conjured him up most distastefully. True, she might have made a more lamentable choice; a silly lordling, or a hero of scandals; but if a gentlemanly official was of stabler mould, he failed to harmonize quite so well with the idea of a creature like Tony. Perhaps Mr. Redworth also failed in something. Where was the man fitly to mate her! Mr. Redworth, however, was manly and trustworthy, of the finest Saxon type in build and in character. He had great qualities, and his excess of scrupulousness was most pitiable.

She read: 'The wisest thing a waif can do.' It bore a sound of desperation. Avowedly Tony had accepted him without being in love. Or was she masking the passion? No: had it been a case of love, she would have written very differently to her friend.

Lady Dunstane controlled the pricking of the wound inflicted by Diana's novel exercise in laconics where the fullest flow was due to tenderness, and despatched felicitations upon the text of the initial line: 'Wonders are always happening.' She wrote to hide vexation beneath surprise; naturally betraying it. 'I must hope and pray that you have not been precipitate.' Her curiosity to inspect the happiest of men, the most genuine part of her letter, was expressed coldly.

When she had finished the composition she perused it, and did not recognize herself in her language, though she had been so guarded to cover the wound her Tony dealt their friendship—in some degree injuring their sex. For it might now, after such an example, verily seem that women are incapable of a translucent perfect confidence: their impulses, caprices, desperations, tricks of concealment, trip a heart-whole friendship. Well, to-morrow, if not to-day, the tripping may be expected! Lady Dunstane resigned herself sadly to a lowered view of her Tony's character. This was her unconscious act of reprisal. Her brilliant beloved Tony, dazzling but in beauty and the gifted mind, stood as one essentially with the common order of women. She wished to be settled, Mr. Warwick proposed, and for the sake of living at The Crossways she accepted him—she, the lofty scorner of loveless marriages! who had said—how many times! that nothing save love excused it! She degraded their mutual high standard of womankind. Diana was in eclipse, full three parts. The bulk of the gentlemanly official she had chosen obscured her. But I have written very carefully, thought Lady Dunstane, dropping her answer into the post-bag. She had, indeed, been so care ful, that to cloak her feelings, she had written as another person. Women with otiose husbands have a task to preserve friendship.

Redworth carried his burden through the frosty air at a pace to melt icicles in Greenland. He walked unthinkingly, right ahead, to the red West, as he discovered when pausing to consult his watch. Time was left to return at the same pace and dress for dinner; he swung round and picked up remembrances of sensations he had strewn by the way. She knew these woods; he was walking in her footprints; she was engaged to be married. Yes, his principle, never to ask a woman to marry him, never to court her, without bank-book assurance of his ability to support her in cordial comfort, was right. He maintained it, and owned himself a donkey for having stuck to it. Between him and his excellent principle there was war, without the slightest division. Warned of the danger of losing her, he would have done the same again, confessing himself donkey for his pains. The principle was right, because it was due to the woman. His rigid adherence to the principle set him belabouring his donkey-ribs, as the proper due to himself. For he might have had a chance, all through two Winters. The opportunities had been numberless. Here, in this beech wood; near that thornbush; on the juniper slope; from the corner of chalk and sand in junction, to the corner of clay and chalk; all the length of the wooded ridge he had reminders of her presence and his priceless chances: and still the standard of his conduct said No, while his heart bled.

He felt that a chance had been. More sagacious than Lady Dunstane, from his not nursing a wound, he divined in the abruptness of Diana's resolution to accept a suitor, a sober reason, and a fitting one, for the wish that she might be settled. And had he spoken!— If he had spoken to her, she might have given her hand to him, to a dishonourable brute! A blissful brute. But a worse than donkey. Yes, his principle was right, and he lashed with it, and prodded with it, drove himself out into the sour wilds where bachelordom crops noxious weeds without a hallowing luminary, and clung to it, bruised and bleeding though he was.

The gentleness of Lady Dunstane soothed him during the term of a visit that was rather like purgatory sweetened by angelical tears. He was glad to go, wretched in having gone. She diverted the incessant conflict between his insubordinate self and his castigating, but avowedly sovereign, principle. Away from her, he was the victim of a flagellation so dire that it almost drove him to revolt against the lord he served, and somehow the many memories at Copsley kept him away. Sir Lukin, when speaking of Diana's 'engagement to that fellow Warwick,' exalted her with an extraordinary enthusiasm, exceedingly hard for the silly beast who had lost her to bear. For the present the place dearest to Redworth of all places on earth was unendurable.

Meanwhile the value of railway investments rose in the market, fast as asparagus-heads for cutting: a circumstance that added stings to reflection. Had he been only a little bolder, a little less the fanatical devotee of his rule of masculine honour, less the slave to the letter of success . . . . But why reflect at all? Here was a goodly income approaching, perhaps a seat in Parliament; a station for the airing of his opinions—and a social status for the wife now denied to him. The wife was denied to him; he could conceive of no other. The tyrant-ridden, reticent, tenacious creature had thoroughly wedded her in mind; her view of things had a throne beside his own, even in their differences. He perceived, agreeing or disagreeing, the motions of her brain, as he did with none other of women; and this it is which stamps character on her, divides her from them, upraises and enspheres. He declined to live with any other of the sex.

Before he could hear of the sort of man Mr. Warwick was—a perpetual object of his quest—the bridal bells had rung, and Diana Antonia Merion lost her maiden name. She became the Mrs. Warwick of our footballing world.

Why she married, she never told. Possibly, in amazement at herself subsequently, she forgot the specific reason. That which weighs heavily in youth, and commits us to desperate action, will be a trifle under older eyes, to blunter senses, a more enlightened understanding. Her friend Emma probed for the reason vainly. It was partly revealed to Redworth, by guess-work and a putting together of pieces, yet quite luminously, as it were by touch of tentacle-feelers—one evening that he passed with Sir Lukin Dunstane, when the lachrymose ex-dragoon and son of Idlesse, had rather more than dined.

CHAPTER VI.
THE COUPLE

Six months a married woman, Diana came to Copsley to introduce her husband. They had run over Italy: 'the Italian Peninsula,' she quoted him in a letter to Lady Dunstane: and were furnishing their London house. Her first letters from Italy appeared to have a little bloom of sentiment. Augustus was mentioned as liking this and that in the land of beauty. He patronized Art, and it was a pleasure to hear him speak upon pictures and sculptures; he knew a great deal about them. 'He is an authority.' Her humour soon began to play round the fortunate man, who did not seem, to the reader's mind, to bear so well a sentimental clothing. His pride was in being very English on the Continent, and Diana's instances of his lofty appreciations of the garden of Art and Nature, and statuesque walk through it, would have been more amusing if her friend could have harmonized her idea of the couple. A description of 'a bit of a wrangle between us' at Lucca, where an Italian post-master on a journey of inspection, claimed a share of their carriage and audaciously attempted entry, was laughable, but jarred. Would she some day lose her relish for ridicule, and see him at a distance? He was generous, Diana, said she saw fine qualities in him. It might be that he was lavish on his bridal tour. She said he was unselfish, kind, affable with his equals; he was cordial to the acquaintances he met. Perhaps his worst fault was an affected superciliousness before the foreigner, not uncommon in those days. 'You are to know, dear Emmy, that we English are the aristocracy of Europeans.' Lady Dunstane inclined to think we were; nevertheless, in the mouth of a 'gentlemanly official' the frigid arrogance added a stroke of caricature to his deportment. On the other hand, the reports of him gleaned by Sir Lukin sounded favourable. He was not taken to be preternaturally stiff, nor bright, but a goodish sort of fellow; good horseman, good shot, good character. In short, the average Englishman, excelling as a cavalier, a slayer, and an orderly subject.

That was a somewhat elevated standard to the patriotic Emma. Only she would never have stipulated for an average to espouse Diana. Would he understand her, and value the best in her? Another and unanswered question was, how could she have condescended to wed with an average? There was transparently some secret not confided to her friend.

He appeared. Lady Dunstane's first impression of him recurred on his departure. Her unanswered question drummed at her ears, though she remembered that Tony's art in leading him out had moderated her rigidly judicial summary of the union during a greater part of the visit. But his requiring to be led out, was against him. Considering the subjects, his talk was passable. The subjects treated of politics, pictures, Continental travel, our manufactures, our wealth and the reasons for it —excellent reasons well-weighed. He was handsome, as men go; rather tall, not too stout, precise in the modern fashion of his dress, and the pair of whiskers encasing a colourless depression up to a long, thin, straight nose, and closed lips indicating an aperture. The contraction of his mouth expressed an intelligence in the attitude of the firmly negative.

The lips opened to smile, the teeth were faultless; an effect was produced, if a cold one—the colder for the unparticipating northern eyes; eyes of that half cloud and blue, which make a kind of hueless grey, and are chiefly striking in an authoritative stage. Without contradicting, for he was exactly polite, his look signified a person conscious of being born to command: in fine, an aristocrat among the 'aristocracy of Europeans.' His differences of opinion were prefaced by a 'Pardon me,' and pausing smile of the teeth; then a succinctly worded sentence or two, a perfect settlement of the dispute. He disliked argumentation. He said so, and Diana remarked it of him, speaking as, a wife who merely noted a characteristic. Inside his boundary, he had neat phrases, opinions in packets. Beyond it, apparently the world was void of any particular interest. Sir Lukin, whose boundary would have shown a narrower limitation had it been defined, stood no chance with him. Tory versus Whig, he tried a wrestle, and was thrown. They agreed on the topic of Wine. Mr. Warwick had a fine taste in wine. Their after-dinner sittings were devoted to this and the alliterative cognate theme, equally dear to the gallant ex-dragoon, from which it resulted that Lady Dunstane received satisfactory information in a man's judgement of him. 'Warwick is a clever fellow, and a thorough man of the world, I can tell you, Emmy.' Sir Lukin further observed that he was a gentlemanly fellow. 'A gentlemanly official!' Diana's primary dash of portraiture stuck to him, so true it was! As for her, she seemed to have forgotten it. Not only did she strive to show him to advantage by leading him out; she played second to him; subserviently, fondly; she quite submerged herself, content to be dull if he might shine; and her talk of her husband in her friend's blue-chamber boudoir of the golden stars, where they had discussed the world and taken counsel in her maiden days, implied admiration of his merits. He rode superbly: he knew Law: he was prepared for any position: he could speak really eloquently; she had heard him at a local meeting. And he loved the old Crossways almost as much as she did. 'He has promised me he will never ask me to sell it,' she said, with a simpleness that could hardly have been acted.

When she was gone, Lady Dunstane thought she had worn a mask, in the natural manner of women trying to make the best of their choice; and she excused her poor Tony for the artful presentation of him at her own cost. But she could not excuse her for having married the man. Her first and her final impression likened him to a house locked up and empty: a London house conventionally furnished and decorated by the upholsterer, and empty of inhabitants. How a brilliant and beautiful girl could have committed this rashness, was the perplexing riddle: the knottier because the man was idle: and Diana had ambition; she despised and dreaded idleness in men. Empty of inhabitants even to the ghost! Both human and spiritual were wanting. The mind contemplating him became reflectively stagnant.

I must not be unjust! Lady Dunstane hastened to exclaim, at a whisper that he had at least proved his appreciation of Tony; whom he preferred to call Diana, as she gladly remembered: and the two were bound together for a moment warmly by her recollection of her beloved Tony's touching little petition: 'You will invite us again?' and then there had flashed in Tony's dear dark eyes the look of their old love drowning. They were not to be thought of separately. She admitted that the introduction to a woman of her friend's husband is crucially trying to him: he may well show worse than he is. Yet his appreciation of Tony in espousing her, was rather marred by Sir

Lukin's report of him as a desperate admirer of beautiful woman. It might be for her beauty only, not for her spiritual qualities! At present he did not seem aware of their existence. But, to be entirely just, she had hardly exhibited them or a sign of them during the first interview: and sitting with his hostess alone, he had seized the occasion to say, that he was the happiest of men. He said it with the nearest approach to fervour she had noticed. Perhaps the very fact of his not producing a highly favourable impression, should be set to plead on his behalf. Such as he was, he was himself, no simulator. She longed for Mr. Redworth's report of him.

Her compassion for Redworth's feelings when beholding the woman he loved another man's wife, did not soften the urgency of her injunction that he should go speedily, and see as much of them as he could. 'Because,' she gave her reason, 'I wish Diana to know she has not lost a single friend through her marriage, and is only one the richer.'

Redworth buckled himself to the task. He belonged to the class of his countrymen who have a dungeon-vault for feelings that should not be suffered to cry abroad, and into this oubliette he cast them, letting them feed as they might, or perish. It was his heart down below, and in no voluntary musings did he listen to it, to sustain the thing. Grimly lord of himself, he stood emotionless before the world. Some worthy fellows resemble him, and they are called deep-hearted. He was dungeon- deep. The prisoner underneath might clamour and leap; none heard him or knew of him; nor did he ever view the day. Diana's frank: 'Ah, Mr. Redworth, how glad I am to see you!' was met by the calmest formalism of the wish for her happiness. He became a guest at her London house, and his report of the domesticity there, and notably of the lord of the house, pleased Lady Dunstane more than her husband's. He saw the kind of man accurately, as far as men are to be seen on the surface; and she could say assentingly, without anxiety: 'Yes, yes,' to his remarks upon Mr. Warwick, indicative of a man of capable head in worldly affairs, commonplace beside his wife. The noble gentleman for Diana was yet unborn, they tacitly agreed. Meantime one must not put a mortal husband to the fiery ordeal of his wife's deserts, they agreed likewise. 'You may be sure she is a constant friend,' Lady Dunstane said for his comfort; and she reminded herself subsequently of a shade of disappointment at his imperturbable rejoinder: 'I could calculate on it.' For though not at all desiring to witness the sentimental fit, she wished to see that he held an image of Diana:—surely a woman to kindle poets and heroes, the princes of the race; and it was a curious perversity that the two men she had moved were merely excellent, emotionless, ordinary men, with heads for business. Elsewhere, out of England, Diana would have been a woman for a place in song, exalted to the skies. Here she had the destiny to inflame Mr. Redworth and Mr. Warwick, two railway Directors, bent upon scoring the country to the likeness of a child's lines of hop-scotch in a gravel-yard.

As with all invalids, the pleasure of living backward was haunted by the tortures it evoked, and two years later she recalled this outcry against the Fates. She would then have prayed for Diana to inflame none but such men as those two. The original error was; of course, that rash and most inexplicable marriage, a step never alluded to by the driven victim of it. Lady Dunstane heard rumours of dissensions. Diana did not mention them. She spoke of her husband as unlucky in railway ventures, and of a household necessity for money, nothing further. One day she wrote of a Government appointment her husband had received, ending the letter: 'So there is the end of our troubles.' Her friend rejoiced, and afterward looking back at her satisfaction, saw the dire beginning of them.

Lord Dannisburgh's name, as one of the admirers of Mrs. Warwick, was dropped once or twice by Sir Lukin. He had dined with the Warwicks, and met the eminent member of the Cabinet at their table. There is no harm in admiration, especially on the part of one of a crowd observing a star. No harm can be imputed when the husband of a beautiful woman accepts an appointment from the potent Minister admiring her. So Lady Dunstane thought, for she was sure of Diana to her inmost soul. But she soon perceived in Sir Lukin that the old Dog-world was preparing to yelp on a scent. He of his nature belonged to the hunting pack, and with a cordial feeling for the quarry, he was quite with his world in expecting to see her run, and readiness to join the chase. No great scandal had occurred for several months. The world was in want of it; and he, too, with a very cordial feeling for the quarry, piously hoping she would escape, already had his nose to ground, collecting testimony in the track of her. He said little to his wife, but his world was getting so noisy that he could not help half pursing his lips, as with the soft whistle of an innuendo at the heels of it. Redworth was in America, engaged in carving up that hemisphere. She had no source of information but her husband's chance gossip; and London was death to her; and Diana, writing faithfully twice a week, kept silence as to Lord Dannisburgh, except in naming him among her guests. She wrote this, which might have a secret personal signification: 'We women are the verbs passive of the alliance; we have to learn, and if we take to activity, with the best intentions, we conjugate a frightful disturbance. We are to run on lines, like the steam-trains, or we come to no station, dash to fragments. I have the misfortune to know I was born an active. I take my chance.'

Once she coupled the names of Lord Larrian and Lord Dannisburgh, remarking that she had a fatal attraction for antiques.

The death of her husband's uncle and illness of his aunt withdrew her to The Crossways, where she remained nursing for several months, reading diligently, as her letters showed, and watching the approaches of the destroyer. She wrote like her former self, subdued by meditation in the presence of that inevitable. The world ceased barking. Lady Dunstane could suppose Mr. Warwick to have now a reconciling experience of his wife's noble qualities. He probably did value them more. He spoke of her to Sir Lukin in London with commendation. 'She is an attentive nurse.' He inherited a considerable increase of income when he and his wife were the sole tenants of The Crossways, but disliking the house, for reasons hard to explain by a man previously professing to share her attachment to it, he wished to sell or let the place, and his wife would do neither. She proposed to continue living in their small London house rather than be cut off from The Crossways, which, he said, was ludicrous: people should live up to their position; and he sneered at the place, and slightly wounded her, for she was open to a wound when the cold fire of a renewed attempt at warmth between them was crackling and showing bits of flame, after she had given proof of her power to serve. Service to himself and his relatives affected him. He deferred to her craze for The Crossways, and they lived in a larger London house, 'up to their position,' which means ever a trifle beyond it, and gave choice dinner-parties to the most eminent. His jealousy slumbered. Having ideas of a seat in Parliament at this period, and preferment superior to the post he held, Mr. Warwick deemed it sagacious to court the potent patron Lord Dannisburgh could be; and his wife had his interests at heart, the fork-tongued world said. The cry revived. Stories of Lord D. and Mrs. W. whipped the hot pursuit. The moral repute of the great Whig lord and the beauty of the lady composed inflammable material.

'Are you altogether cautious?' Lady Dunstane wrote to Diana; and her friend sent a copious reply: 'You have the fullest right to ask your Tony anything, and I will answer as at the Judgement bar. You allude to Lord Dannisburgh. He is near what Dada's age would have been, and is, I think I can affirm, next to my dead father and my Emmy, my dearest friend. I love him. I could say it in the streets without shame; and you do not imagine me shameless. Whatever his character in his younger days, he can be honestly a woman's friend, believe me. I see straight to his heart; he has no disguise; and unless I am to suppose that marriage is the end of me, I must keep him among my treasures. I see him almost daily; it is not possible to think I can be deceived; and as long as he does me the honour to esteem my poor portion of brains by coming to me for what he is good enough to call my counsel, I shall let the world wag its tongue. Between ourselves, I trust to be doing some good. I know I am of use in various ways. No doubt there is a danger of a woman's head being turned, when she reflects that a powerful Minister governing a kingdom has not considered her too insignificant to advise him; and I am sensible of it. I am, I assure you, dearest, on my guard against it. That would not attach me to him, as his homely friendliness does. He is the most amiable, cheerful, benignant of men; he has no feeling of an enemy, though naturally his enemies are numerous and venomous. He is full of observation and humour. How he would amuse you! In many respects accord with you. And I should not have a spark of jealousy. Some day I shall beg permission to bring him to Copsley. At present, during the Session, he is too busy, as you know. Me—his "crystal spring of wisdom"—he can favour with no more than an hour in the afternoon, or a few minutes at night. Or I get a pencilled note from the benches of the House, with an anecdote, or news of a Division. I am sure to be enlivened.

'So I have written to you fully, simply, frankly. Have perfect faith in your Tony, who would, she vows to heaven; die rather than disturb it and her heart's beloved.'

The letter terminated with one of Lord Dannisburgh's anecdotes, exciting to merriment in the season of its freshness;—and a postscript of information: 'Augustus expects a mission—about a month; uncertain whether I accompany him.'

Mr. Warwick departed on his mission. Diana remained in London. Lady Dunstane wrote entreating her to pass the month—her favourite time of the violet yielding to the cowslip—at Copsley. The invitation could not be accepted, but the next day Diana sent word that she had a surprise for the following Sunday, and would bring a friend to lunch, if Sir Lukin would meet them at the corner of the road in the valley leading up to the heights, at a stated hour.

Lady Dunstane gave the listless baronet his directions, observing: 'It's odd, she never will come alone since her marriage.'

'Queer,' said he of the serenest absence of conscience; and that there must be something not, entirely right going on, he strongly inclined to think.

CHAPTER VII.
THE CRISIS

It was a confirmed suspicion when he beheld Lord Dannisburgh on the box of a four-in-hand, and the peerless Diana beside him, cockaded lackeys in plain livery and the lady's maid to the rear. But Lord Dannisburgh's visit was a compliment, and the freak of his driving down under the beams of Aurora on a sober Sunday morning capital fun; so with a gaiety that was kept alive for the invalid Emma to partake of it, they rattled away to the heights, and climbed them, and Diana rushed to the arms of her friend, whispering and cooing for pardon if she startled her, guilty of a little whiff of blarney:—Lord Dannisburgh wanted so much to be introduced to her, and she so much wanted her to know him, and she hoped to be graciously excused for thus bringing them together, 'that she might be chorus to them!' Chorus was a pretty fiction on the part of the thrilling and topping voice. She was the very radiant Diana of her earliest opening day, both in look and speech, a queenly comrade, and a spirit leaping and shining like a mountain water. She did not seduce, she ravished. The judgement was taken captive and flowed with her. As to the prank of the visit, Emma heartily enjoyed it and hugged it for a holiday of her own, and doating on the beautiful, darkeyed, fresh creature, who bore the name of the divine Huntress, she thought her a true Dian in stature, step, and attributes, the genius of laughter superadded. None else on earth so sweetly laughed, none so spontaneously, victoriously provoked the healthful openness. Her delicious chatter, and her museful sparkle in listening, equally quickened every sense of life. Adorable as she was to her friend Emma at all times, she that day struck a new fountain in memory. And it was pleasant to see the great lord's admiration of this wonder. One could firmly believe in their friendship, and his winning ideas from the abounding bubbling well. A recurrent smile beamed on his face when hearing and observing her. Certain dishes provided at the table were Diana's favourites, and he relished them, asking for a second help, and remarking that her taste was good in that as in all things. They lunched, eating like boys. They walked over the grounds of Copsley, and into the lanes and across the meadows of the cowslip, rattling, chatting, enlivening the frosty air, happy as children biting to the juices of ripe apples off the tree. But Tony was the tree, the dispenser of the rosy gifts. She had a moment of reflection, only a moment, and Emma felt the pause as though a cloud had shadowed them and a spirit had been shut away. Both spoke of their happiness at the kiss of parting. That melancholy note at the top of the wave to human hearts conscious of its enforced decline was repeated by them, and Diana's eyelids blinked to dismiss a tear.

'You have no troubles?' Emma said.

'Only the pain of the good-bye to my beloved,' said Diana. 'I have never been happier—never shall be! Now you know him you think with me? I knew you would. You have seen him as he always is—except when he is armed for battle. He is the kindest of souls. And soul I say. He is the one man among men who gives me notions of a soul in men.'

The eulogy was exalted. Lady Dunstane made a little mouth for Oh, in correction of the transcendental touch, though she remembered their foregone conversations upon men—strange beings that they are!—and understood Diana's meaning.

'Really! really! honour !' Diana emphasized her extravagant praise, to print it fast. 'Hear him speak of Ireland.'

'Would he not speak of Ireland in a tone to catch the Irishwoman?'

'He is past thoughts of catching, dearest. At that age men are pools of fish, or what you will: they are not anglers. Next year, if you invite us, we will come again.'

'But you will come to stay in the Winter?'

'Certainly. But I am speaking of one of my holidays.'

They kissed fervently. The lady mounted; the grey and portly lord followed her; Sir Lukin flourished his whip, and Emma was left to brood over her friend's last words: 'One of my holidays.' Not a hint to the detriment of her husband had passed. The stray beam balefully illuminating her marriage slipped from her involuntarily. Sir Lukin was troublesome with his ejaculations that evening, and kept speculating on the time of the arrival of the four-in-hand in London; upon which he thought a great deal depended. They had driven out of town early, and if they drove back late they would not be seen, as all the cacklers were sure then to be dressing for dinner, and he would not pass the Clubs. 'I couldn't suggest it,' he said. 'But Dannisburgh's an old hand. But they say he snaps his fingers at tattle, and laughs. Well, it doesn't matter for him, perhaps, but a game of two . . . . Oh! it'll be all right. They can't reach London before dusk. And the cat's away.'

'It's more than ever incomprehensible to me how she could have married that man,' said his wife.

'I've long since given it up,' said he.

Diana wrote her thanks for the delightful welcome, telling of her drive home to smoke and solitude, with a new host of romantic sensations to keep her company. She wrote thrice in the week, and the same addition of one to the ordinary number next week. Then for three weeks not a line. Sir Lukin brought news from London that Warwick had returned, nothing to explain the silence. A letter addressed to The Crossways was likewise unnoticed. The supposition that they must be visiting on a round, appeared rational; but many weeks elapsed, until Sir Lukin received a printed sheet in the superscription of a former military comrade, who had marked a paragraph. It was one of those journals, now barely credible, dedicated to the putrid of the upper circle, wherein initials raised sewer-lamps, and Asmodeus lifted a roof, leering hideously. Thousands detested it, and fattened their crops on it. Domesticated beasts of superior habits to the common will indulge themselves with a luxurious roll in carrion, for a revival of their original instincts. Society was largely a purchaser. The ghastly thing was dreaded as a scourge, hailed as a refreshment, nourished as a parasite. It professed undaunted honesty, and operated in the fashion of the worms bred of decay. Success was its boasted justification. The animal world, when not rigorously watched, will always crown with success the machine supplying its appetites. The old dog-world took signal from it. The one-legged devil- god waved his wooden hoof, and the creatures in view, the hunt was uproarious. Why should we seem better than we are? down with hypocrisy, cried the censor morum, spicing the lamentable derelictions of this and that great person, male and female. The plea of corruption of blood in the world, to excuse the public chafing of a grievous itch, is not less old than sin; and it offers a merry day of frisky truant running to the animal made unashamed by another and another stripped, branded, and stretched flat. Sir Lukin read of Mr. and Mrs. W. and a distinguished Peer of the realm. The paragraph was brief; it had a flavour. Promise of more to come, pricked curiosity. He read it enraged, feeling for his wife; and again indignant, feeling for Diana. His third reading found him out: he felt for both, but as a member of the whispering world, much behind the scenes, he had a longing for the promised insinuations, just to know what they could say, or dared say. The paper was not shown to Lady Dunstane. A run to London put him in the tide of the broken dam of gossip. The names were openly spoken and swept from mouth to mouth of the scandalmongers, gathering matter as they flew. He knocked at Diana's door, where he was informed that the mistress of the house was absent. More than official gravity accompanied the announcement. Her address was unknown. Sir Lukin thought it now time to tell his wife. He began with a hesitating circumlocution, in order to prepare her mind for bad news. She divined immediately that it concerned Diana, and forcing him to speak to the point, she had the story jerked out to her in a sentence. It stopped her heart.

The chill of death was tasted in that wavering ascent from oblivion to recollection. Why had not Diana come to her, she asked herself, and asked her husband; who, as usual, was absolutely unable to say. Under compulsory squeezing, he would have answered, that she did not come because she could not fib so easily to her bosom friend: and this he thought, notwithstanding his personal experience of Diana's generosity. But he had other personal experiences of her sex, and her sex plucked at the bright star and drowned it.

The happy day of Lord Dannisburgh's visit settled in Emma's belief as the cause of Mr. Warwick's unpardonable suspicions and cruelty. Arguing from her own sensations of a day that had been like the return of sweet health to her frame, she could see nothing but the loveliest freakish innocence in Diana's conduct, and she recalled her looks, her words, every fleeting gesture, even to the ingenuousness of the noble statesman's admiration of her, for the confusion of her unmanly and unworthy husband. And Emma was nevertheless a thoughtful person; only her heart was at the head of her thoughts, and led the file, whose reasoning was accurate on erratic tracks. All night her heart went at fever pace. She brought the repentant husband to his knees, and then doubted, strongly doubted, whether she would, whether in consideration for her friend she could, intercede with Diana to forgive him. In the morning she slept heavily. Sir Lukin had gone to London early for further tidings. She awoke about midday, and found a letter on her pillow. It was Diana's. Then while her fingers eagerly tore it open, her heart, the champion rider over-night, sank. It needed support of facts, and feared them: not in distrust of that dear persecuted soul, but because the very bravest of hearts is of its nature a shivering defender, sensitive in the presence of any hostile array, much craving for material support, until the mind and spirit displace it, depute it to second them instead of leading.

She read by a dull November fog-light a mixture of the dreadful and the comforting, and dwelt upon the latter in abandonment, hugged it, though conscious of evil and the little that there was to veritably console.

The close of the letter struck the blow. After bluntly stating that Mr. Warwick had served her with a process, and that he had no case without suborning witnesses, Diana said: 'But I leave the case, and him, to the world. Ireland, or else America, it is a guiltless kind of suicide to bury myself abroad. He has my letters. They are such as I can own to you; and ask you to kiss me—and kiss me when you have heard all the evidence, all that I can add to it, kiss me. You know me too well to think I would ask you to kiss criminal lips. But I cannot face the world. In the dock, yes. Not where I am expected to smile and sparkle, on pain of incurring suspicion if I show a sign of oppression. I cannot do that. I see myself wearing a false grin—your Tony! No, I do well to go. This is my resolution; and in consequence,—my beloved! my only truly loved on earth! I do not come to you, to grieve you, as I surely should. Nor would it soothe me, dearest. This will be to you the best of reasons. It could not soothe me to see myself giving pain to Emma. I am like a pestilence, and let me swing away to the desert, for there I do no harm. I know I am right. I have questioned myself—it is not cowardice. I do not quail. I abhor the part of actress. I should do it well—too well; destroy my soul in the performance. Is a good name before such a world as this worth that sacrifice? A convent and self-quenching;—cloisters would seem to me like holy dew. But that would be sleep, and I feel the powers of life. Never have I felt them so mightily. If it were not for being called on to act and mew, I would stay, fight, meet a bayonet-hedge of charges and rebut them. I have my natural weapons and my cause. It must be confessed that I have also more knowledge of men and the secret contempt—it must be—the best of them entertain for us. Oh! and we confirm it if we trust them. But they have been at a wicked school.

'I will write. From whatever place, you shall have letters, and constant. I write no more now. In my present mood I find no alternative between rageing and drivelling. I am henceforth dead to the world. Never dead to Emma till my breath is gone—poor flame! I blow at a bed-room candle, by which I write in a brown fog, and behold what I am— though not even serving to write such a tangled scrawl as this. I am of no mortal service. In two days I shall be out of England. Within a week you shall hear where. I long for your heart on mine, your dear eyes. You have faith in me, and I fly from you!—I must be mad. Yet I feel calmly reasonable. I know that this is the thing to do. Some years hence a grey woman may return, to hear of a butterfly Diana, that had her day and disappeared. Better than a mewing and courtseying simulacrum of the woman—I drivel again. Adieu. I suppose I am not liable to capture and imprisonment until the day when my name is cited to appear. I have left London. This letter and I quit the scene by different routes—I would they were one. My beloved! I have an ache—I think I am wronging you. I am not mistress of myself, and do as something within me, wiser, than I, dictates.—You will write kindly. Write your whole heart. It is not compassion I want, I want you. I can bear stripes from you. Let me hear Emma's voice—the true voice. This running away merits your reproaches. It will look like—. I have more to confess: the tigress in me wishes it were! I should then have a reckless passion to fold me about, and the glory infernal, if you name it so, and so it would be— of suffering for and with some one else. As it is, I am utterly solitary, sustained neither from above nor below, except within myself, and that is all fire and smoke, like their new engines.—I kiss this miserable sheet of paper. Yes, I judge that I have run off a line—and what a line! which hardly shows a trace for breathing things to follow until they feel the transgression in wreck. How immensely nature seems to prefer men to women!—But this paper is happier than the writer.

'Your TONY.'

That was the end. Emma kissed it in tears. They had often talked of the possibility of a classic friendship between women, the alliance of a mutual devotedness men choose to doubt of. She caught herself accusing Tony of the lapse from friendship. Hither should the true friend have flown unerringly.

The blunt ending of the letter likewise dealt a wound. She reperused it, perused and meditated. The flight of Mrs. Warwick! She heard that cry- fatal! But she had no means of putting a hand on her. 'Your Tony.' The coldness might be set down to exhaustion: it might, yet her not coming to her friend for counsel and love was a positive weight in the indifferent scale. She read the letter backwards, and by snatches here and there; many perusals and hours passed before the scattered creature exhibited in its pages came to her out of the flying threads of the web as her living Tony, whom she loved and prized and was ready to defend gainst the world. By that time the fog had lifted; she saw the sky on the borders of milky cloudfolds. Her invalid's chill sensitiveness conceived a sympathy in the baring heavens, and lying on her sofa in the drawing-room she gained strength of meditative vision, weak though she was to help, through ceasing to brood on her wound and herself. She cast herself into her dear Tony's feelings; and thus it came, that she imagined Tony would visit The Crossways, where she kept souvenirs of her father, his cane, and his writing-desk, and a precious miniature of him hanging above it, before leaving England forever. The fancy sprang to certainty; every speculation confirmed it.

Had Sir Lukin been at home she would have despatched him to The Crossways at once. The West wind blew, and gave her a view of the Downs beyond the Weald from her southern window. She thought it even possible to drive there and reach the place, on the chance of her vivid suggestion, some time after nightfall; but a walk across the room to try her forces was too convincing of her inability. She walked with an ebony silver-mounted stick, a present from Mr. Redworth. She was leaning on it when the card of Thomas Redworth was handed to her.

CHAPTER VIII.
IN WHICH IS EXHIBITED HOW A PRACTICAL MAN AND A DIVINING WOMAN LEARN TO RESPECT ONE ANOTHER

'You see, you are my crutch,' Lady Dunstane said to him,—raising the stick in reminder of the present.

He offered his arm and hurriedly informed her, to dispose of dull personal matter, that he had just landed. She looked at the clock. 'Lukin is in town. You know the song: "Alas, I scarce can go or creep While Lukin is away." I do not doubt you have succeeded in your business over there. Ah! Now I suppose you have confidence in your success. I should have predicted it, had you come to me.' She stood, either musing or in weakness, and said abruptly: 'Will you object to lunching at one o'clock?'

'The sooner the better,' said Redworth. She had sighed: her voice betrayed some agitation, strange in so serenely-minded a person.

His partial acquaintance with the Herculean Sir Lukin's reputation in town inspired a fear of his being about to receive admission to the distressful confidences of the wife, and he asked if Mrs. Warwick was well. The answer sounded ominous, with its accompaniment of evident pain: 'I think her health is good.'

Had they quarrelled? He said he had not heard a word of Mrs. Warwick for several months.

'I—heard from her this morning,' said Lady Dunstane, and motioned him to a chair beside the sofa, where she half reclined, closing her eyes. The sight of tears on the eyelashes frightened him. She roused herself to look at the clock. 'Providence or accident, you are here,' she said. 'I could not have prayed for the coming of a truer' man. Mrs. Warwick is in great danger . . . . You know our love. She is the best of me, heart and soul. Her husband has chosen to act on vile suspicions— baseless, I could hold my hand in the fire and swear. She has enemies, or the jealous fury is on the man—I know little of him. He has commenced an action against her. He will rue it. But she . . . you understand this of women at least;—they are not cowards in all things! —but the horror of facing a public scandal: my poor girl writes of the hatefulness of having to act the complacent—put on her accustomed self! She would have to go about, a mark for the talkers, and behave as if nothing were in the air-full of darts! Oh, that general whisper!—it makes a coup de massue—a gale to sink the bravest vessel: and a woman must preserve her smoothest front; chat, smile—or else!—Well, she shrinks from it. I should too. She is leaving the country.'

'Wrong!' cried Redworth.

'Wrong indeed. She writes, that in two days she will be out of it. Judge her as I do, though you are a man, I pray. You have seen the hunted hare. It is our education—we have something of the hare in us when the hounds are full cry. Our bravest, our best, have an impulse to run. "By this, poor Wat far off upon a hill." Shakespeare would have the divine comprehension. I have thought all round it and come back to him. She is one of Shakespeare's women: another character, but one of his own:—another Hermione! I dream of him—seeing her with that eye of steady flame. The bravest and best of us at bay in the world need an eye like his, to read deep and not be baffled by inconsistencies.'

Insensibly Redworth blinked. His consciousness of an exalted compassion for the lady was heated by these flights of advocacy to feel that he was almost seated beside the sovereign poet thus eulogized, and he was of a modest nature.

'But you are practical,' pursued Lady Dunstane, observing signs that she took for impatience. 'You are thinking of what can be done. If Lukin were here I would send him to The Crossways without a moment's delay, on the chance, the mere chance:—it shines to me! If I were only a little stronger! I fear I might break down, and it would be unfair to my husband. He has trouble enough with my premature infirmities already. I am certain she will go to The Crossways. Tony is one of the women who burn to give last kisses to things they love. And she has her little treasures hoarded there. She was born there. Her father died there. She is three parts Irish—superstitious in affection. I know her so well. At this moment I see her there. If not, she has grown unlike herself.'

'Have you a stout horse in the stables?' Redworth asked.

'You remember the mare Bertha; you have ridden her.'

'The mare would do, and better than a dozen horses.' He consulted his watch. 'Let me mount Bertha, I engage to deliver a letter at The Crossways to-night.'

Lady Dunstane half inclined to act hesitation in accepting the aid she sought, but said: 'Will you find your way?'

He spoke of three hours of daylight and a moon to rise. 'She has often pointed out to me from your ridges where The Crossways lies, about three miles from the Downs, near a village named Storling, on the road to Brasted.

The house has a small plantation of firs behind it, and a bit of river— rare for Sussex—to the right. An old straggling red brick house at Crossways, a stone's throw from a fingerpost on a square of green: roads to Brasted, London, Wickford, Riddlehurst. I shall find it. Write what you have to say, my lady, and confide it to me. She shall have it to- night, if she's where you suppose. I 'll go, with your permission, and take a look at the mare. Sussex roads are heavy in this damp weather, and the frost coming on won't improve them for a tired beast. We haven't our rails laid down there yet.'

'You make me admit some virtues in the practical,' said Lady Dunstane; and had the poor fellow vollied forth a tale of the everlastingness of his passion for Diana, it would have touched her far less than his exact memory of Diana's description of her loved birthplace.

She wrote:

> 'I trust my messenger to tell you how I hang on you. I see my ship making for the rocks. You break your Emma›s heart. It will be the second wrong step. I shall not survive it. The threat has made me incapable of rushing to you, as I might have had strength to do yesterday. I am shattered, and I wait panting for Mr. Redworth's return with you. He has called, by accident, as we say. Trust to him. If ever heaven was active to avert a fatal mischance it is to- day. You will not stand

against my supplication. It is my life I cry for. I have no more time. He starts. He leaves me to pray— like the mother seeing her child on the edge of the cliff. Come. This is your breast, my Tony? And your soul warns you it is right to come. Do rightly. Scorn other counsel—the coward's. Come with our friend—the one man known to me who can be a friend of women.

'Your EMMA.'

Redworth was in the room. 'The mare 'll do it well,' he said. 'She has had her feed, and in five minutes will be saddled at the door.'

'But you must eat, dear friend,' said the hostess.

'I'll munch at a packet of sandwiches on the way. There seems a chance, and the time for lunching may miss it.'

'You understand . . . ?'

'Everything, I fancy.'

'If she is there!'

'One break in the run will turn her back.'

The sensitive invalid felt a blow in his following up the simile of the hunted hare for her friend, but it had a promise of hopefulness. And this was all that could be done by earthly agents, under direction of spiritual, as her imagination encouraged her to believe.

She saw him start, after fortifying him with a tumbler of choice Bordeaux, thinking how Tony would have said she was like a lady arming her knight for battle. On the back of the mare he passed her window, after lifting his hat, and he thumped at his breast-pocket, to show her where the letter housed safely. The packet of provision bulged on his hip, absurdly and blessedly to her sight, not unlike the man, in his combination of robust serviceable qualities, as she reflected during the later hours, until the sun fell on smouldering November woods, and sensations of the frost he foretold bade her remember that he had gone forth riding like a huntsman. His great-coat lay on a chair in the hall, and his travelling-bag was beside it. He had carried it up from the valley, expecting hospitality, and she had sent him forth half naked to weather a frosty November night! She called in the groom, whose derision of a great-coat for any gentleman upon Bertha, meaning work for the mare, appeased her remorsefulness. Brisby, the groom, reckoned how long the mare would take to do the distance to Storling, with a rider like Mr. Redworth on her back. By seven, Brisby calculated, Mr. Redworth would be knocking at the door of the Three Ravens Inn, at Storling, when the mare would have a decent grooming, and Mr. Redworth was not the gentleman to let her be fed out of his eye. More than that, Brisby had some acquaintance with the people of the inn. He begged to inform her ladyship that he was half a Sussex man, though not exactly born in the county; his parents had removed to Sussex after the great event; and the Downs were his first field of horse-exercise, and no place in the world was like them, fair weather or foul, Summer or Winter, and snow ten feet deep in the gullies. The grandest air in England, he had heard say.

His mistress kept him to the discourse, for the comfort of hearing hard bald matter-of-fact; and she was amused and rebuked by his assumption that she must be entertaining an anxiety about master's favourite mare. But, ah! that Diana had delayed in choosing a mate; had avoided her disastrous union with perhaps a more imposing man, to see the true beauty of masculine character in Mr. Redworth, as he showed himself to-day. How could he have doubted succeeding? One grain more of faith in his energy, and Diana might have been mated to the right husband for her—an open- minded clear-faced English gentleman. Her speculative ethereal mind clung to bald matter-of-fact to-day. She would have vowed that it was the sole potentially heroical. Even Brisby partook of the reflected rays, and he was very benevolently considered by her. She dismissed him only when his recounting of the stages of Bertha's journey began to fatigue her and deaden the medical efficacy of him and his like. Stretched on the sofa, she watched the early sinking sun in South-western cloud, and the changes from saffron to intensest crimson, the crown of a November evening, and one of frost.

Redworth struck on a southward line from chalk-ridge to sand, where he had a pleasant footing in familiar country, under beeches that browned the ways, along beside a meadowbrook fed by the heights, through pines and across deep sand-ruts to full view of weald and Downs. Diana had been with him here in her maiden days. The coloured back of a coach put an end to that dream. He lightened his pocket, surveying the land as he munched. A favourable land for rails: and she had looked over it: and he was now becoming a wealthy man: and she was a married woman straining the leash. His errand would not bear examination, it seemed such a desperate long shot. He shut his inner vision on it, and pricked forward. When the burning sunset shot waves above the juniper and yews behind him, he was far on the weald, trotting down an interminable road. That the people opposing railways were not people of business, was his reflection, and it returned persistently: for practical men, even the most devoted among them, will think for themselves; their army, which is the rational, calls them to its banners, in opposition to the sentimental; and Redworth joined it in the abstract, summoning the horrible state of the roads to testify against an enemy wanting almost in common humaneness. A slip of his excellent stepper in one of the half-frozen pits of the highway was the principal cause of his confusion of logic; she was half on her knees. Beyond the market town the roads were so bad that he quitted them, and with the indifference of an engineer, struck a line of his own Southeastward over fields and ditches, favoured by a round horizon moon on his left. So for a couple of hours he went ahead over rolling fallow land to the meadow-flats and a pale shining of freshets; then hit on a lane skirting the water, and reached an amphibious village; five miles from Storling, he was informed, and a clear traverse of lanes, not to be mistaken, 'if he kept a sharp eye open.' The sharpness of his eyes was divided between the sword-belt of the starry Hunter and the shifting lanes that zig-tagged his course below. The Downs were softly illuminated; still it amazed him to think of a woman like Diana Warwick having an attachment to this district, so hard of yield, mucky, featureless, fit but for the rails she sided with her friend in detesting. Reasonable women, too! The moon, stood high on her march as he entered Storling. He led his good beast to the stables of The Three Ravens, thanking her and caressing her. The ostler conjectured from the look of the mare that he had been out with the hounds and lost his way. It appeared to Redworth singularly, that near the ending of a wild goose chase, his plight was pretty well described by the fellow. However, he had to knock at the door of The Crossways now, in the silent night time, a certainly empty house, to his fancy. He fed on a snack of cold meat and tea, standing, and set forth, clearly directed, 'if he kept a sharp eye open.' Hitherto he had proved his capacity, and he rather smiled at the repetition of the formula to him, of all men. A turning to the right was taken, one to the left, and through the churchyard, out of the gate, round to the right, and on.

By this route, after an hour, he found himself passing beneath the bare chestnuts of the churchyard wall of Storling, and the sparkle of the edges of the dead chestnut-leaves at his feet reminded him of the very ideas he had entertained when treading them. The loss of an hour strung him to pursue the chase in earnest, and he had a beating of the heart as he thought that it might be serious. He recollected thinking it so at Copsley. The long ride, and nightfall, with nothing in view, had obscured his mind to the possible behind the thick obstruction of the probable; again the possible waved its marsh- light. To help in saving her from a fatal step, supposing a dozen combinations of the conditional mood, became his fixed object, since here he was—of that there was no doubt; and he was not here to play the fool, though the errand were foolish. He entered the churchyard, crossed the shadow of the tower, and hastened along the path, fancying he beheld a couple of figures vanishing before him. He shouted; he hoped to obtain directions from these natives: the moon was bright, the gravestones legible; but no answer came back, and the place appeared to belong entirely to the dead. 'I've frightened them,' he thought. They left a queerish sensation in his frame. A ride down to Sussex to see ghosts would be an odd experience; but an undigested dinner of tea is the very grandmother of ghosts; and he accused it of confusing him, sight and mind. Out of the gate, now for the turning to the right, and on. He turned. He must have previously turned wrongly somewhere— and where? A light in a cottage invited him to apply for the needed directions. The door was opened by a woman, who had never heard tell of The Crossways, nor had her husband, nor any of the children crowding round them. A voice within ejaculated: 'Crassways!' and soon upon the grating of a chair, an old man, whom the woman named her lodger, by way of introduction, presented himself with his hat on, saying: 'I knows the spot they calls Crassways,' and he led. Redworth understood the intention that a job was to be made of it, and submitting, said: 'To the right, I think.' He was bidden to come along, if he wanted 'they Crassways,' and from the right they turned to the left, and further sharp round, and on to a turn, where the old man, otherwise incommunicative, said: 'There, down thik theer road, and a post in the middle.'

'I want a house, not a post!' roared Redworth, spying a bare space.

The old man despatched a finger travelling to his nob. 'Naw, there's ne'er a house. But that's crassways for four roads, if it 's crassways, you wants.'

They journeyed backward. They were in such a maze of lanes that the old man was master, and Redworth vowed to be rid of him at the first cottage. This, however, they were long in reaching, and the old man was promptly through the garden-gate, hailing the people and securing 'information, before Redworth could well hear. He smiled at the dogged astuteness of a dense-headed old creature determined to establish a claim to his fee. They struck a lane sharp to the left.

'You're Sussex?' Redworth asked him, and was answered: 'Naw; the Sheers.'

Emerging from deliberation, the old man said: 'Ah'm a Hampshireman.'

'A capital county!'

'Heigh!' The old man heaved his chest. 'Once!'

'Why, what has happened to it?'

'Once it were a capital county, I say. Hah! you asks me what have happened to it. You take and go and look at it now. And down heer'll be no better soon, I tells 'em. When ah was a boy, old Hampshire was a proud country, wi' the old coaches and the old squires, and Harvest Homes, and Christmas merryings.—Cutting up the land! There's no pride in livin' theer, nor anywhere, as I sees, now.'

'You mean the railways.'

'It's the Devil come up and abroad ower all England!' exclaimed the melancholy ancient patriot.

A little cheering was tried on him, but vainly. He saw with unerring distinctness the triumph of the Foul Potentate, nay his personal appearance 'in they theer puffin' engines.' The country which had produced Andrew Hedger, as he stated his name to be, would never show the same old cricketing commons it did when he was a boy. Old England, he declared, was done for.

When Redworth applied to his watch under the brilliant moonbeams, he discovered that he had been listening to this natural outcry of a decaying and shunted class full three-quarters of an hour, and The Crossways was not in sight. He remonstrated. The old man plodded along. 'We must do as we're directed,' he said.

Further walking brought them to a turn. Any turn seemed hopeful. Another turn offered the welcome sight of a blazing doorway on a rise of ground off the road. Approaching it, the old man requested him to 'bide a bit,' and stalked the ascent at long strides. A vigorous old fellow. Redworth waited below, observing how he joined the group at the lighted door, and, as it was apparent, put his question of the whereabout of The Crossways. Finally, in extreme impatience, he walked up to the group of spectators. They were all, and Andrew Hedger among them, the most entranced and profoundly reverent, observing the dissection of a pig.

Unable to awaken his hearing, Redworth jogged his arm, and the shake was ineffective until it grew in force.

'I've no time to lose; have they told you the way?'

Andrew Hedger yielded his arm. He slowly withdrew his intent fond gaze from the fair outstretched white carcase, and with drooping eyelids, he said: 'Ah could eat hog a solid hower!'

He had forgotten to ask the way, intoxicated by the aspect of the pig; and when he did ask it, he was hard of understanding, given wholly to his last glimpses.

Redworth got the directions. He would have dismissed Mr. Andrew Hedger, but there was no doing so. 'I'll show ye on to The Crossways House,' the latter said, implying that he had already earned something by showing him The Crossways post.

'Hog's my feed,' said Andrew Hedger. The gastric springs of eloquence moved him to discourse, and he unburdened himself between succulent pauses. 'They've killed him early. He 's fat; and he might ha' been fatter. But he's fat. They've got their Christmas ready, that they have. Lord! you should see the chitterlings, and—the sausages hung up to and along the beams. That's a crown for any dwellin'! They runs 'em round the top of the room—it's like a May-day wreath in old times. Home-fed hog! They've a treat in store, they have. And snap your fingers at the world for many a long day. And the hams! They cure their own hams at that house. Old style! That's what I say of a hog. He's good from end to end, and beats a Christian hollow. Everybody knows it and owns it.'

Redworth was getting tired. In sympathy with current conversation, he said a word for the railways: they would certainly make the flesh of swine cheaper, bring a heap of hams into the market. But Andrew Hedger remarked with contempt that he had not much opinion of foreign hams: nobody, knew what they fed on. Hog, he said, would feed on anything, where there was no choice they had wonderful stomachs for food. Only, when they had a choice, they left the worst for last, and home-fed filled them with stuff to make good meat and fat 'what we calls prime bacon.' As it is not right to damp a native enthusiasm, Redworth let him dilate on his theme, and mused on his boast to eat hog a solid hour, which roused some distant classic recollection: — an odd jumble.

They crossed the wooden bridge of a flooded stream.

'Now ye have it,' said the hog-worshipper; 'that may be the house, I reckon.'

A dark mass of building, with the moon behind it, shining in spires through a mound of firs, met Redworth's gaze. The windows all were blind, no smoke rose from the chimneys. He noted the dusky square of green, and the finger-post signalling the centre of the four roads. Andrew Hedger repeated that it was The Crossways house, ne'er a doubt. Redworth paid him his expected fee, whereupon Andrew, shouldering off, wished him a hearty good night, and forthwith departed at high pedestrian pace, manifestly to have a concluding look at the beloved anatomy.

There stood the house. Absolutely empty! thought Redworth. The sound of the gate-bell he rang was like an echo to him. The gate was unlocked. He felt a return of his queer churchyard sensation when walking up the garden-path, in the shadow of the house. Here she was born: here her father died: and this was the station of her dreams, as a girl at school near London and in Paris. Her heart was here. He looked at the windows facing the Downs with dead eyes. The vivid idea of her was a phantom presence, and cold, assuring him that the bodily Diana was absent. Had Lady Dunstane guessed rightly, he might perhaps have been of service!

Anticipating the blank silence, he rang the house-bell. It seemed to set wagging a wearyful tongue in a corpse. The bell did its duty to the last note, and one thin revival stroke, for a finish, as in days when it responded livingly to the guest. He pulled, and had the reply, just the same, with the faint terminal touch, resembling exactly a 'There!' at the close of a voluble delivery in the negative. Absolutely empty. He pulled and pulled. The bell wagged, wagged. This had been a house of a witty host, a merry girl, junketting guests; a house of hilarious thunders, lightnings of fun and fancy. Death never seemed more voiceful than in that wagging of the bell.

For conscience' sake, as became a trusty emissary, he walked round to the back of the house, to verify the total emptiness. His apprehensive despondency had said that it was absolutely empty, but upon consideration he supposed the house must have some guardian: likely enough, an old gardener and his wife, lost in deafness double-shotted by sleep! There was no sign of them. The night air waxed sensibly crisper. He thumped the backdoors. Blank hollowness retorted on the blow. He banged and kicked. The violent altercation with wood and wall lasted several minutes, ending as it had begun.

Flesh may worry, but is sure to be worsted in such an argument.

'Well, my dear lady !'—Redworth addressed Lady Dunstane aloud, while driving his hands into his pockets for warmth—'we've done what we could. The next best thing is to go to bed and see what morning brings us.'

The temptation to glance at the wild divinings of dreamy-witted women from the point of view of the practical man, was aided by the intense frigidity of the atmosphere in leading him to criticize a sex not much used to the exercise of brains. 'And they hate railways!' He associated them, in the matter of intelligence, with Andrew Hedger and Company. They sank to the level of the temperature in his esteem—as regarded their intellects. He approved their warmth of heart. The nipping of the victim's toes and finger-tips testified powerfully to that.

Round to the front of the house at a trot, he stood in moonlight. Then, for involuntarily he now did everything running, with a dash up the steps he seized the sullen pendant bell-handle, and worked it pumpwise, till he perceived a smaller bell-knob beside the door, at which he worked piston- wise. Pump and piston, the hurly-burly and the tinkler created an alarm to scare cat and mouse and Cardinal spider, all that run or weave in desolate houses, with the good result of a certain degree of heat to his frame. He ceased, panting. No stir within, nor light. That white stare of windows at the moon was undisturbed.

The Downs were like a wavy robe of shadowy grey silk. No wonder that she had loved to look on them!

And it was no wonder that Andrew Hedger enjoyed prime bacon. Bacon frizzling, fat rashers of real homefed on the fire-none of your foreign- suggested a genial refreshment and resistance to antagonistic elements. Nor was it, granting health, granting a sharp night—the temperature at least fifteen below zero—an excessive boast for a man to say he could go on eating for a solid hour.

These were notions darting through a half nourished gentleman nipped in the frame by a severely frosty night. Truly a most beautiful night! She would have delighted to see it here. The Downs were like floating islands, like fairy-laden vapours; solid, as Andrew Hedger's hour of eating; visionary, as too often his desire!

Redworth muttered to himself, after taking the picture of the house and surrounding country from the sward, that he thought it about the sharpest night he had ever encountered in England. He was cold, hungry, dispirited, and astoundingly stricken with an incapacity to separate any of his thoughts from old Andrew Hedger. Nature was at her pranks upon him.

He left the garden briskly, as to the legs, and reluctantly. He would have liked to know whether Diana had recently visited the house, or was expected. It could be learnt in the morning; but his mission was urgent and he on the wings of it. He was vexed and saddened.

Scarcely had he closed the garden-gate when the noise of an opening window arrested him, and he called. The answer was in a feminine voice, youngish, not disagreeable, though not Diana's.

He heard none of the words, but rejoined in a bawl: 'Mrs. Warwick!—Mr. Redworth!'

That was loud enough for the deaf or the dead.

The window closed. He went to the door and waited. It swung wide to him; and O marvel of a woman's divination of a woman! there stood Diana.